CLAIMING OF THE DEERFOOT

A WESTERN DUO

CLAIMING
OF THE
DEERFOOT

A WESTERN DUO

PETER DAWSON

Thorndike Press • Chivers Press
Thorndike, Maine USA Bath, England

This Large Print edition is published by Thorndike Press, USA and by Chivers Press, England.

Published in 2001 in the U.S. by arrangement with Golden West Literary Agency.

Published in 2001 in the U.K. by arrangement with Golden West Literary Agency.

U.S. Hardcover 0-7862-2125-9   (Western Series Edition)
U.K. Hardcover 0-7540-4531-5   (Chivers Large Print)
U.K. Softcover 0-7540-4532-3   (Camden Large Print)

The text of this Large Print edition is unabridged.
Other aspects of the book may vary from the original edition.

Set in 16 pt. Plantin by Rick Gundberg.

Printed in the United States on permanent paper.

British Library Cataloguing in Publication Data available

Library of Congress Cataloging-in-Publication Data

Dawson, Peter, 1907–
    Claiming of the Deerfoot : a western duo / Peter Dawson.
       p. cm.
    ISBN 0-7862-2125-9 (lg. print : hc : alk. paper)
    1. Western stories. I. Large type books. II. Title.
PS3507.A848 C58 2001   00-066614

TABLE OF CONTENTS

Barbed Wire 7

Claiming of the Deerfoot 129

BARBED WIRE

Chapter One

"Cowman's Challenge"

Ed Nugent eyed his foreman coldly. Ben Starr, ordinarily a hard-bitten, tough-looking rider, was a sorry sight right now. He was breathing hard, there was a lump on his jaw, and his lower lip was cut and swollen. His left sleeve was ripped halfway to the shoulder, and a bloody bandanna was wrapped around his right hand. One other thing Nugent noticed as his ramrod swung from the saddle of his winded horse: Starr had lost his gun. His holster was empty.

"What did you do, fall off the rim?" Nugent said acidly.

He knew it was more than anything that trivial. An hour and a half ago he had sent Starr up into the near hills to investigate a plume of smoke showing in the direction of Ford's abandoned homestead shack. He'd given Starr specific orders to warn off anyone he found on Ford's place, if necessary to kick them off. For last fall Nugent had cleared the immediate range of both squat-

9

ters and homesteaders, and he had no intention of having to do it again.

Just now Ben Starr was a moment catching his breath. When he did, he blurted out: "How was I to know he was packin' an iron under his shirt?"

Nugent's brows lifted a trifle. "Now don't tell me you got caught cold on a draw, Ben," he said ironically. "Who was this gent you ran into?"

"A lanky tow-head jasper with a Texas drawl. Claims he owns Ford's place." Starr gripped the wrist above his injured hand.

Nugent saw this. "Shot your gun out of your fist, did he?"

"I was takin' my time." Starr bridled. "First thing I knew he slid his hand under his shirt and filled it. Got in a lucky shot before I knew what he was up to."

"Break any bones?"

"No. It'll heal in a few days."

"What happened then?" Nugent asked.

"He invited me to climb down." Starr glared at the five other 'punchers who had followed the boss down here to the corral as he had come in fast along the trail. "What could I do with a bum paw? Besides, he's plenty big."

Nugent was even more surprised at this than he had been at Starr's admission of being beaten on the draw. For if Ben was handy with a gun, he was even more a tough scrapper — as tough a one as Nugent knew.

"Is he alone?" Nugent asked.

"Far as I know."

Nugent nodded briefly to the others. "Let's ride," he said in a clipped, flat tone.

The five Bar Cross crewmen smiled as they turned away to the corral, knowing from what had happened last fall that they might have some fun before the morning was over. Hadn't the boss driven Ford out of the country? Hadn't he made it so tough for the other homesteaders up there in the hills that they'd moved off their places?

Forty minutes later Ed Nugent and his five men rode in through the break in Ford's railyard fence and up on a tall, flat-bodied stranger who stood indolently leaning against one post of the well cupola. As Nugent pulled his horse in to a stand close to the well, the stranger pushed erect.

" 'Mornin', gents," he drawled. "Light and have a cup of java?"

Nugent had warned the rest to let him do the talking. Now he made no immediate reply, instead looked down at the stranger from his superior height with a cold and direct glance. Nugent was a big man both in name

11

and in stature, as tall as the man he now faced and a good bit heavier. The expensiveness of his outfit made quite a contrast to the plainness of the stranger's, whose waist overalls were faded and patched at the insides of the knees and whose boots were unpolished and worn over at the heels. Still, something about this Texan's easy drawl and the half smile on his hawkish face made Ed Nugent weigh carefully what he was to say.

Finally he said it, a flat-worded: "Stranger, this country's been closed to homesteaders. You'll have to move on."

The stranger's smile vanished. Sober, his lean face was still pleasant, good-natured. "That's what Ford tried to tell me," he drawled. "Only I looked it up at a government Land Office. Ford was wrong. This is open country, and he had clear title to the lay-out, so I came up to look it over. It'll do."

"Have you given Ford any money for it yet?" Nugent asked. "Because, if you haven't, you'd better save your *dinero*."

The stranger shrugged. "No, I didn't exactly pay out anything for it except enough to cover his bet."

Nugent frowned. "Bet?"

"Yeah. I won this lay-out from Ford in a stud game down in Amarillo."

"Then you wouldn't be losin' anything if

you don't stay," Nugent said deliberately. "We'll give you an hour to gather your possibles and clear out."

Now the stranger was smiling again. Only this time the smile wasn't pleasant, and the look in his warm brown eyes had changed so that they were cold, uncompromising. "You must be Nugent. I heard on the way up here that you cast a mighty wide shadow. Now I was tellin' myself only a while ago how you couldn't be as bad a neighbor as they said you was . . . how, maybe, you'd think twice before you told me to move on. Because I kind o' like this place, Nugent. I aim to stay. And I aim to be friendly."

"One of you light and get his iron," Nugent said, without taking his glance from the stranger. "A couple more of you carry his junk out of that shack and set it afire." As he spoke, he drew a .45 from his low-thonged holster.

The stranger's brows lifted as he stared down the barrel of the Colt. For a moment it was so quiet that the whisper of a faint breeze through a nearby pine sounded loud.

Three of the men behind Nugent were swinging to the ground when the stranger's voice broke the tension. He said loudly: "Bill, lay your sights on the one with the iron! Don't shoot till he does, or till I give the word!"

Nugent stiffened in surprise. His glance left

the stranger, whipping to the corners of the shack, then to its door. He saw no one.

"Bill's at the window there where you see that Winchester," the stranger drawled. "I forgot to tell you about Bill. He's my partner."

Nugent looked at the window then, saw the blued barrel of a carbine aimed almost squarely at him, and cursed Ben Starr for not keeping his eyes open. His men, behind, also saw what was in the window. The three out of their saddles froze, motionless. The other pair were careful not to move their hands.

"You can toss that hogleg across here, Nugent," the stranger said flatly. "Bill's got a hair-trigger temper. You'd better move fast before he wings you."

Ed Nugent sat rock-still a moment, holding back his anger. Then, because he never crowded his luck, he lowered the Colt and tossed it onto a patch of grass ahead of his horse.

"Keep an eye on the rest until they've shucked out their irons, Bill!" the stranger called, and sauntered over to pick up Nugent's gun. As he stood erect, the last of Nugent's riders carefully drew his gun from holster and let it fall to the hard-packed ground at his feet.

The stranger nodded and, Nugent's .45

carelessly in hand at his side, walked over to the cabin window. He reached out, pushed the window sash back, and took hold of the rifle's barrel swinging the weapon out of the opening. He looked down at it, his angular face slashed with a wide grin.

"Nice goin', Bill," he said. He glanced at Nugent, holding out the rifle. "Me and Bill always travel together. He makes a good sidekick. By the way, Nugent. Since I'm stayin' on, you'd better know my handle. It's Lance . . . Jim Lance."

Nugent's handsome face had darkened as he saw the simple ruse this Jim Lance had used to outwit him. Behind him, one of his men breathed a salty oath. Nugent didn't see it, but this man was standing half-concealed and out of line with Lance. He made the mistake of reaching down for his gun a moment later.

Nugent saw Lance rock the six-gun into line. The next instant it exploded. Nugent's pony shied violently, and the gun lying under the Bar Cross 'puncher's hand jumped a foot out of reach as Lance's slug hit it.

As Nugent steadied his nervous horse, Lance was saying: "You birds catch on slow. I don't push around easy. Now, if you'll climb aboard those jug-head bronc's real fast and clear out, I won't get the notion to part your hair with any of this lead."

Nugent's shame was heightened by the speed with which his men mounted and left the yard, leaving him sitting his horse alone there. With a baleful glance back that showed him the last of his five men going out through the hole in the fence, the Bar Cross owner faced Lance once more.

"Think you'll make this stick?" he asked.

"It's stuck so far. I never think too far ahead," was Lance's slow answer.

"Now's a good time to start."

With that, Nugent reined his horse around and followed his men away.

Jim Lance let his breath out in a long, relieved sigh. He'd had his second lucky break of the morning, and common sense told him that next time — and there would be a next time — he might not have things so much his own way. He'd seen Nugent and the others coming up the trail and hastily made preparations, not at all sure that they would net him anything. Luckily, his bluff had worked.

"Now what?" he breathed as he went out to pick up the five guns lying in the yard.

He couldn't answer that. But he knew he was staying.

CHAPTER TWO

"A NEW OFFENSIVE"

Last night Jim Lance had finished a hard five-day ride shortly after dark and felt a keen disappointment on examining Ford's single-room shack, the fallen-in corral, and the roofless log barn. The shack hadn't been much to look at, a cracker-box, tar-paper, and slab cubicle with a wooden bunk in one corner, a cracked cast-iron stove in the other, and a packing-box chair standing next to the stove. Aside from these meager furnishings, the only other things in the room had been three faded calendars and a tattered coyote pelt nailed to the wall over the bunk. The pack rats had moved in with Jim as he cooked his late meal on the stove, so he'd thrown his blankets under a pine out in the yard and slept there.

Before he had dropped off to sleep he'd decided to start back early in the morning. It must have been a hunch, he had thought then, that had made him tell his boss back home he was taking a week's *pasear* up into

17

the Superstitions after antelope; he hadn't even asked for his pay. Instinctively he hadn't expected this thing to pan out, hadn't burned all his bridges behind him. After all, the deed Ford had thrown into the pot that last hand of the game down in Amarillo a week ago had covered only a fifty dollar bet. And after the game, Ford had admitted the deed wasn't even worth fifty.

"It's a nice enough little lay-out," was the way the homesteader had put it. "But I couldn't buck a range hog and a pack o' crooked county commissioners. That's a big-brand country up there. They don't waste much time on the little feller."

"You've proved up on this lay-out?" Jim had asked.

"Oh, sure." Ford had been positive of that. "They let me alone long enough to do that because I was workin' for wages for one of 'em. But the minute I got some money ahead and started workin' on my own, they ran me out. Better forget it, Lance."

So, remembering that conversation, Jim Lance had last night wished he *had* forgotten the matter. Even if he could manage to stay on here, the place didn't look like much.

But this morning he had found it different. From the pine-knobbed knoll behind the cabin, he had looked out across the small

18

downward valley and seen the lush grass greening there with spring still weeks away. He'd seen the stream that snaked across the lower meadow and the sleek fat cattle that had broken through Ford's single-wire fence to feed. He could follow the line of the fence and see that it included all but the upper end of the valley.

There and then Jim had changed his mind. This was a likely-looking place, and he was staying. No more of this riding for any outfit at thirty a month and found. He was past twenty-seven, and it was about time he settled down. Here was a chance to run his own brand. This was a sweet bit of land to start on, good grass, water, and timber. The land maps showed the country west and north to be open range. With the creek so handy, he could raise three crops of alfalfa a year. In five years' time he'd be running enough cattle to need an extra hand on the place. Best of all, he'd already saved enough, upwards of four hundred dollars, to get a good start.

But he had barely finished a breakfast of jerky and pan bread and had started thinking about how he could make the shack more comfortable when Nugent's foreman appeared. Jim hadn't wanted to scrap with Ben Starr, but the man had asked for a licking. He'd tried to be peaceable with Nugent, too.

But they hadn't given him a chance.

So his — "Now what?" — had him stumped. Common sense told him that he'd lose in any open fight with Nugent. Hadn't Nugent started to burn down the shack? Wouldn't he burn it down the first time he found it empty? What could be gained by bucking an outfit as big as the Bar Cross?

Still, Jim knew he was going to stay, knew he was going to make this place his home. He'd already decided on his brand. It would be the Broad Arrow. Sort of went with his name.

Jim spent the next two hours finishing his inspection of the place and beginning the repair of the corral. Afterward, he rode in to the upper end of the meadow and saw from there another cabin less than a mile above and centering an upper widening of the hill fold. He went through his sagging, single-wire fence and rode on up to that cabin. It was empty, but obviously hadn't been for long. It was, Jim decided, the home of another homesteader who had been driven out along with Ford late last fall.

Beyond that cabin he came to a well-used trail and, on impulse, followed it a mile or so down out of the hills to find himself within sight of a town. Ford had mentioned a town, Rimrock. This must be it. He rode on about two more miles and into the upper end of Rimrock's wide street, finding the settlement prettier than most he knew, with a lot of the houses freshly painted, the yards well-kept, and the walks shaded with cottonwood and locust just beginning to come in leaf. Rimrock was different from the towns Jim had seen lately, for his country edged the desert; big trees, grassy yards, and fresh paint were as scarce down there as running water.

The farther he went along the street the more certain he became that he was going to stay on Ford's place, that he liked this country. He came to the stores and was once again favorably impressed. Their windows weren't dusty and filled with faded posters, empty boxes, and cartons; they were clean and displayed merchandise that was for sale and not being used as decoration.

He had ridden on a few rods before he noticed a knot of men gathered on the north, the right-hand, walk, and he idly wondered what they were doing there as his glance ran beyond them. A moment later, as he came closer, he was looking at them again, now seeing that they were watching a man nailing a sheet of paper to the side of a single-story building that marked a break in the long line of wooden store awnings. When he was closer still, he could read the gilt legend lettered on the half-glass door of that small building:

Henry Ashworth
Sheriff, Real Estate, Mining Properties

Under slack rein, Jim's pony had slowed to a walk. He came abreast the crowd, and the chestnut finally lazed to a stand, head toward the crowd.

At that moment, someone over there said something. Immediately the men turned and stared at Jim as those at the center of the crowd moved back to open a lane across the walk. Finally those nearest the building stepped aside. There stood Ed Nugent.

There was a smile on the Bar Cross man's face, and his glance was full on Jim. Alongside him was a fat man from whose vest hung a sheriff's star brightly reflecting the sunlight.

"Get down and take a look at this, Lance!" called Nugent.

Warily Jim studied the faces of the men nearest. They showed him no hostility, only an awed interest. If Nugent had set a trap, Jim didn't yet know what it was. Finally he put the chestnut on in to the tie rail and swung easily to the ground, looping his reins over the pole and ducking under it to step up onto the walk. As he moved, he was keenly aware of the weight of the holster against his thigh. It was rare for him to carry a gun openly, but, when Nugent's foreman had called this morning, he had taken belt and holster from his blanket roll and cinched them on.

Nugent was watching him all this time. "No one's goin' to bite you, Lance," he drawled now.

Jim ignored the bite of the man's words as he sauntered in between the two ranks of men.

Again Nugent spoke: "Curtis, you and Pope and Roberts take a good look, too. Then get together with Lance here and see what you can do about it!"

A wide smile on his face, ignoring Jim, he turned away and pushed out through the crowd and went down the walk. A few re-pressed laughs came from several of the watchers as the sheriff nodded to the notice posted on the wall and told Jim: "Come right ahead, stranger. Better read it careful."

Jim gave the fat man a steady impassive glance, until the other's eyes shifted and moved off him. Then, stepping up to the wall, he read the bold print on the notice.

HOMESTEAD OWNERS
The Commissioners of Soldad County hereby declare that it shall be unlawful for any landowner to enclose less than a

section of land with the accepted legal single-strand fence. Any land tract comprising less than a section, within the limits of Soldad County, must hereafter be enclosed by a fence of at least six strands of barbed wire. In such cases, ready access for range animals must be furnished through said fences to any stream, pond, or tank enclosed by the wire.

> Signed: Edward Nugent, Chairman
> Philip Ross
> Harvey Wright
> Sidney Gant

Jim read the notice twice, gradually taking in what it was to mean to him, roughly calculating the cost of fencing his homestead with six strands of barbed wire and finally realizing that it would take most, if not all, of his money.

As he looked away from the paper, a slow rage beginning to mount in him, the sheriff said piously: "Now I'm a man to turn a deal whenever I can, stranger. If you're figurin' on putting up some fence, I'll sell you the wire at a good discount. Three percent, say?"

Jim fixed the man with a hard stare. "Beat it, tin star," he drawled tonelessly. "You're in the way."

Ashworth's jowled face turned red, and he blustered: "Watch out who you're orderin' around!"

Jim took a half step toward the sheriff.

The look on the law man's face became uncertain, a little afraid. "You watch your step, stranger!" he growled, and backed away. Then, as Jim's stare stayed on him, he glowered at the crowd. "All right, clear the walk!" he called harshly. And with that he turned his back on Jim, opened the door to his office, and disappeared inside.

A chorus of loud guffaws came from the crowd, and it began breaking up. Jim knew he'd made an enemy of the sheriff and regretted it now that his anger had cooled a trifle. Still, he had disliked the fat law man since his first glimpse of him; that dislike had hardened under the knowledge that Ashworth was probably nothing but another understrapper of Nugent's.

CHAPTER THREE

"PARTNERSHIP"

Jim swung around, intending to go out to his horse. But he found his way blocked by a short-coupled man whose battered Stetson was pushed onto the back of a brick-red thatch of hair. Beyond this man along the now cleared walk waited two others. The redhead's stare was belligerent. He stood with boots planted wide apart and hands knotted on hips. Jim stopped and looked down at him, and all at once the smaller man was saying hotly: "I'm Red Curtis. You sure did me one hell of a favor by crossin' Nugent!"

Jim remembered Nugent's advising Curtis to read the notice and said mildly, regret in his voice: "Didn't I!"

"They bluffed Ford and the rest. But so far me and a couple others have stuck. If you hadn't come along, they'd've let us alone. Now they won't! They'll use this to crowd us all out!"

"Feller," Jim said contritely, "I'm like the

26

fiddler when his last string busted. I'm sure sorry to break up the party."

His mildness and sincerity brought a change to Curtis's face. The redhead's anger vanished before a good-natured grin. "Shucks," he said, "let's go buy a drink. It ain't your fault you wouldn't let Nugent push you around. And it was good listenin' when you told off that fat fool they sold us last election for a sheriff." He half turned, indicating the two men standing beyond, waiting. "This is Ralph Pope, and here's Mike Roberts. They're due for the same treatment you and me are gettin'."

Jim shook hands with the homesteaders. Pope was a mustached, graying man wearing bib overalls. Mike Roberts seemed to be of Curtis's approximate age, around thirty. He was tall, cadaverous, and had a dour face and the look of a 'puncher who had rarely eaten enough to fill his shad belly.

"Red, I'm huntin' me a job," Roberts said. "Six wires around my chunk o' land would be more than the place is worth."

"I know," Red Curtis answered, and once more his square face took on a dogged anger.

"The drinks are on me," Jim said. "Where do we put our elbows?"

They found the Hillside empty except for the bartender and swamper and had the bar to themselves as Red called for a bottle of rye. They were silent over the first drink. It was as they poured the second that Jim queried: "That your place above Ford's, Curtis?"

"It's mine," Ralph Pope said. "Me and the wife and kids have been livin' in town over the winter. I've got me a job at the feed mill."

"I'm right north of Ralph, and Mike's place is above mine," Red explained. He shook his head and heaved a slow sigh. "It sure looked like a nice set-up for a while. Good feed, plenty of water, and room to move any way we wanted outside our fences. If Ford had only stayed, we might've made it stick. But he went soft on liquor and cards. The minute Nugent started crackin' the whip, he jumped. Jumped clean out of the country!"

"Nugent got in here and collected his commissioners mighty fast to pass that rulin'," Jim said.

"All he had to do was sign it and have that joker of a sheriff post it," Red explained. "They put it through last fall and have been holdin' it over our heads in case we started really workin' our lay-outs. What did you do to Nugent, Lance? He was madder'n a tick-bit bull when he hit town. And I saw Ben Starr sneakin' in to see the sawbones. He had a lump on his jaw and a bad hand."

"Had a little argument with him," Jim said. "He was. . . ."

Abruptly he broke off, frowning as he stared vacantly at Curtis. The redhead was about to ask what was wrong when Jim said quickly: "You mean to tell me that our four lay-outs string out next to each other up that valley?"

"Yeah," Red answered. "Why?"

"Our boundaries meet?" Jim asked.

Red nodded. "Sure. What if they do?"

Jim downed his drink, looked at the three homesteaders and made sure the barkeeper was out of hearing. Then he spoke in a low voice: "Stop me if I'm wrong on this. You say our boundaries touch all the way through. That means our four places, thrown together, would add up to an even section. Now that new law says that any place under a section has to put up a six-wire fence. Suppose our four places were thrown together and deeded over to one man?"

Pope was first in seeing what he meant. "Go on, friend," he breathed. "It listens good so far."

"We could throw together all our wire," Jim continued. "Instead of it bein' a single-strand fence, we could make it double, maybe triple by layin' out a little cash. We could all move onto one place and pool our money and cattle

29

on whatever shares we decide on. That way, we'd be running a fair-size lay-out with the deed to all four quarter sections in one name."

Red Curtis's fist suddenly hit the bar top with a slam that made the apron at the back end of the counter look up quickly. "Lance, you've got somethin' here!"

"We could do that," Mike Roberts said mournfully. "But sure as shootin' they'd change the rulin' when they saw what we were up to."

"They couldn't. Not without hurting someone they don't mean to," Jim said. "If this country's anything like the one I come from, nobody but the big augurs hold title to more than a section of land. They don't fence even that much in most cases, with all this open country to turn their critters onto."

"That's a fact," Pope put in. "I can name you at least six big brands that won't run but a section of deeded land."

Red Curtis's face was showing a stronger excitement. "It'll work," he said. "And right now I'm puttin' in my say. We're deedin' our places over to Lance." He gave Jim a steady look after a glance at the others. "I got my ideas on what happened up there at your place this mornin', Lance. Nugent was sore. It takes some rilin' to make him get after anyone the way he got after you. And Ben Starr looked to me like he'd been through a threshin' machine and come out feet first. Any man that can whip Starr and make Nugent take water is good enough to look after my interest in this thing."

"Unh-uh," Jim said flatly. "You don't even know me. I might have thought all this out beforehand and be tryin' to swindle you. Or I might even be workin' for Nugent, for all you know."

Red smiled thinly. "What I said still goes. If Pope and Mike here want to write out their private agreements with you, that's up to them. As for me, I'll sign my piece over to you right now and know I'm makin' a good deal."

"That goes for me, too," Roberts put in. He added solemnly: "Mister, we been waitin' for someone to call Ed Nugent's bluff. So far you're the only gent that's had sand enough in his craw to do it."

Pope was slower in making up his mind, and, after Roberts had spoken, the other two looked at him. His aging, lined face took on color as he realized they were noticing his hesitation. "It ain't myself I'm thinkin' of," he blurted out finally. "It's the missus and the kids. I don't want to get them mixed up in any trouble. Besides, I got this job, and I hate to let it go on a long shot like this. You fellers got nothin' to lose. You don't know how it is to have to feed a family of five. If I was alone, it'd be different."

"No one's blamin' you, Ralph," Red said. But even for this assurance, his homely face was clouded with worry.

They stood without speaking for a brief interval, Pope nervously fingering his half-empty shot glass and not looking up at the others. At the back of the barn-like room a big wall clock ticked loudly, and they could hear the steady swish of the swamper's broom as he swept the floor around the poker lay-outs in the back.

It was Jim who broke the uneasy silence. "I've got a little money laid away, Pope," he said. "Supposin' you sell me your quarter section outright. But only until we've settled this thing, once and for all. When it's over, I'll sell it back at what I paid for it."

Pope looked at Jim, and there was humble gratitude and relief in his eyes. "That's mighty white of you, Lance. I. . . ." He got out that much before his voice balled up on him.

"Then it's settled," Red declared.

"Only after we've put a few things in writin' before a notary," said Jim. He grinned, adding: "I don't want the three of you after my scalp a year or so from now after I've run out on you."

"When you run, there won't be anything left to hang around for," Red drawled. "We'll get everything ironed out about what we put on paper."

They had a drink on it.

CHAPTER FOUR

"A NEW RULING"

On the afternoon of the twelfth day after Jim Lance had ridden to Rimrock, Ed Nugent called an unscheduled meeting of the county commissioners. Although it was past closing time, they met as usual in the small directors' room on the second floor over the bank.

Harvey Wright, who ran the oldest and second largest brand in the county, was the last to arrive. He was a small, grizzled man who made up for his lack of stature with a fine blend of shrewdness and dogged honesty to give him a solid reputation. As he opened the door and came into the room that was already smoke-fogged from three half-consumed cigars, he glanced coolly at Ed Nugent.

"All right, let's get on with it," he said curtly, tossing his hat onto a chair. "And it'd better be good, Nugent. I'm too old for these long rides. It's twenty miles in and twenty back. Now what've you got on your mind?" He took the chair at the end of the table facing the Bar Cross man.

Nugent began in what he thought was a careful way, knowing very well the older man's dislike for him. "I wanted you here before I told the others, Wright. As the oldest member of the commission, you. . . ."

"Lay off the fancy talk," the older rancher cut in. He took out his watch and looked at it. "It's exactly nine minutes to four, and I never eat later than seven. Which means we'll have to wind this up in a hurry."

Ed Nugent breathed a scarcely perceptible sigh and came closer to the point. "It's a matter of direct violation of the ruling we passed on fencing in homesteads. I'm asking the commission, as a body, to swear out warrants on four men . . . Red Curtis, Ralph Pope, Mike Roberts, and this stranger, Jim Lance."

Harvey Wright's face lost its stern cast and took on a half smile. "Lance? He's the gent that tossed Starr around, ain't he?"

Nugent nodded. "He is. But he's also in with the three others on this violation."

Philip Ross, who owned the feed mill, said: "I don't know what you're drivin' at, Ed, but Ralph Pope is as honest a man as I have reason to know. A good worker, too."

"Most of this is Lance's fault," Nugent was quick to say. "He's the one who thought it out, and I'd as soon name him wholly responsible for what's happened."

"What has happened?" demanded Wright. He coughed and grimaced in distaste at the thickening blue haze in the room. Finally he rose and opened a window that looked out on the alley. Although he chewed tobacco, he didn't smoke it.

"What's happened?" Nugent echoed, his expression indignant. "Those four have thrown their homesteads together and recorded them in Lance's name under his ownership. They're putting up a two-strand fence. It's a flat violation of our ruling, a dodge to get around buying the wire to put up legal fences."

"How's that?"

"Their quarter sections thrown together make a full section," Nugent explained. "Our ruling applied only to land of under a section."

Harvey Wright's smile broadened, and he laughed softly. "Not bad," he drawled. "This Lance must have a head on his shoulders." He sobered with difficulty. "Well, what do we do about it? Far as I can see, we passed this new fence law only so you'd be able to run those small outfits off your end of the range, Nugent. It don't matter to me or anyone else but you, whether they stay or leave. And it shouldn't matter to you. It'll take a lot more crowdin' before your steers go gaunt."

Nugent ignored the sarcasm and played his trump card. "Remember the deal we made, Wright?" he asked. "You voted with me on this fence law, and I voted your way on the county posting that timber above your place to keep loggers out."

Wright frowned and cleared his throat nervously, showing how squarely Nugent's reminder had hit him. "What do you want us to do?" he growled.

"Henry Ashworth is supposed to approve all changes of property deeds," Nugent said. "Up to now, he's let Fall, the recorder, put his name to these transactions."

"Because he's too busy to do it himself," Wright put in.

"That's probably true," agreed Nugent. "In this case, Red Curtis is a friend of Fall's and evidently told Fall to keep the change of deeds under his hat. Nobody, not even the sheriff, knew of the switch in titles to one name until one of my men spotted the changes that were being made in fences up that valley. I sent this man over to see Curtis, and he came back with the story. What I want is an amendment to that ruling to read something like this." Nugent took a paper from his pocket and glanced at it. " 'The aforesaid fence law shall apply to all property of under one section as recorded on the day this notice was posted, March Eighteenth. Any appeal to this amendment will be considered by the county commission.' "

"You're expecting us to turn down any appeal Curtis or his partners might make?" Ross asked.

"Naturally," was Nugent's reply. He saw that the feed-mill owner was about to protest further and added hastily: "It's the work of this commission to protect the interests of the county. We protected Wright here, when a logging outfit threatened to strip the hills above his place. Years back, I understand you had the survey for the north county road changed, the location moved half a mile out of line so it would pass your mill, Ross. That was an expense to the county. This ruling I'm asking for isn't. The purpose of this board is to protect the interests of citizens of this county. Yours have been protected. Now I'm asking you to protect mine."

The fourth man in the room, Sidney Gant, spoke for the first time. "Ed, you're growin' a little big for your britches. I can remember once, when I busted out the seams of mine. First thing I knew, I'd near lost 'em. All I say is . . . watch your step. Now let's quit the talk and get this in the books."

Of them all, Gant's word possibly bore the greatest weight. He owned more property in

Rimrock than any other man and, along with Wright, usually ran the county board pretty much his own way. Just now he was yielding some ground to Nugent, the newest member, but yielding it with a warning and an unspoken admission that Nugent had outthought the others. For, singly, neither he nor Wright or Ross would have approved such a measure as Nugent was forcing through.

The amended notice was posted on the wall of the sheriff's office some twenty minutes later. Ralph Pope, on his way home from work at the feed mill later, saw it. He ate a hurried supper and at dark rode out to Ford's homestead cabin, which the others had made their headquarters, to break the news.

As the older man told them of the new ruling, Jim's lips gradually hardened to a thin, tight line. When Pope had finished, Jim listened to Red's furious outburst and to Mike's opinion that they'd better quit the whole thing. Then, instinctively, they looked at him.

Without a word, he left the cabin's main room, and went into the new slab-walled addition they had built during the past week as a bunkroom. He came back lugging a bulging saddlebag and put it on the table by the lamp. Digging down into it, he brought out a package wrapped in brown paper. Red had brought it out yesterday from the post office.

Breaking open the package, Jim tossed what it held to the table.

It was a tightly rolled bundle of banknotes. It represented every dollar Jim Lance had to his name. His pay from his old job, his savings.

"There ought to be close to five hundred there," he said. "I warned you I was puttin' more in this besides what work I could turn out. We'll buy enough wire to beat that rulin'. Then we'll see what Nugent can think up next."

CHAPTER FIVE

"CUT FENCES"

The fences were finished by mid-April, in time so that Jim, Red, and Mike could work at calving on Harvey Wright's lay-out, twenty miles to the north. Wright had offered Red jobs for the three of them one day in town. When Red had thanked him, the old rancher's reply was a gruff: "Shucks, I'm doin' myself more of a favor than you or your sidekicks. I'm payin' only twenty and found for the time I need you. It may be two weeks or a month, dependin' on what the crop is. Take it or leave it."

They took it gladly, and the work lasted eighteen days. During that time they spent four sleepless nights fighting to save part of Wright's calf crop caught in the higher hills by a late blizzard. It was Jim who made a night ride down to one of Wright's line camps for two double-bitted axes and helped strip enough jack pine that night and the next morning to build a windbreak that saved the half hundred newborn calves from freezing to

41

death in a flimsy pole corral. He and Red and two of Wright's 'punchers fed a roaring fire behind the windbreak all through that day and the next night, until the icy wind died and a quick thaw began.

Later, one of those crewmen who had worked with Jim told Wright: "If it hadn't been for that jasper from Texas, I'd be out of a job right now. I didn't think we had a prayer of savin' them dogies when that storm hit. But this Lance got to work like it was his own beef he was keepin' from freezin'."

The night he paid off the downcountry men, Wright told Red Curtis: "I'm culling out sixty or seventy white-face yearlings and offerin' 'em to the first taker at ten dollars a head. Thought you might be in the market for a good buy, Red."

Red couldn't hide his surprise and eagerness. He turned to Jim and Mike, who stood a few feet away, holding the horses.

"Hear that, boys?" he called.

"We're broke," was Jim's brief but meaningful answer.

Wright ignored the Texan, still speaking to Red. "Your credit's good, Curtis," he said. "I'd charge you interest at six percent."

Red's jaw went a little slack. "Ten a head," he said, only half aloud. "It's a steal at that price."

"Wait'll you get in the business of raisin' your own stuff, waitin' for a good price, and then driving a hundred miles to a railroad only to find out the bottom has dropped from under the market," said Wright. "Did you ever know me to come out on the hind end of a bargain?"

"No," Red admitted. Still, yearlings were worth more than $10 a head. He turned to Jim and Mike again. "How about it?"

Jim handed his reins to Mike and came over. He gave Wright a steady look. "What's the catch?" he asked.

"There ain't any," the rancher said testily.

"Yearlings, even culls, are worth more than ten a head," Jim insisted.

Wright did some quick thinking then, knowing that this tall, soft-spoken man had seen through the flimsy fabric of his trying to return a favor in his roundabout way. "They're worth more than ten right now," he admitted. "But I'm overstocked on yearlings. Another thing. I go by the weather. We've had more snow this past winter than in twenty years. There'll be floods this spring, and we're due for a wet summer. That means hoof rot and sick stuff. My calf crop last year was heavy. I'm only usin' my head in thinnin' the herd to what I figure the range will stand."

"Sounds like sense to me," Mike called

across. His voice was edgy with eagerness.

Jim's look held steadily on Wright a moment longer. He was a proud man, too proud to accept charity. Was Wright doing this to pay them back for working their guts out to save his calves? They'd been paid to do a job and had done it. Or was he telling the truth about wanting to trim down the size of his yearling herd?

Finally Jim made up his mind. "The market on yearlings is fifteen a head. They. . . ."

"Fifteen delivered," Wright cut in.

Jim nodded. "Delivery ought to run two dollars a head, which would make thirteen the price here. We could buy them for that from any outfit near town. But we're after a bargain. We'll offer eleven, if you let us have a hundred head, and sign a note at six percent. You'll have to drive 'em down to our place, or it's no deal."

Wright started to get sore, then had to control his face to check a smile. This Jim Lance was a proud ranny. He'd argued until he'd found a way to take advantage of the bargain without accepting any favors — or so he was making it seem. Here was the kind of trade Harvey Wright liked, and he liked the man with whom he was trading.

So he complained: "How can I spare the men to send those critters down? It'd take two days, and I'm short-handed."

"Knock off fifty cents a head, and we'll drive 'em down ourselves," Jim said with a straight face.

"Fifty cents? That's fifty dollars! I can hire any two men in this country at four dollars a day to do the job."

"That's our offer," Jim drawled. "Take it or leave it."

Wright swore heatedly and looked at Red. "You're sure thrown in with a horse thief!"

Red grinned. "No tellin' what he was before he hit these parts."

"All right, rob me, then," Wright growled. "Only do your own drivin'. I'm too busy to bother goin' into town to hunt up two saddle bums. It's worth fifty dollars to get out of it."

Three days later, as Jim and Red and Mike pushed their hundred-head herd into the upper end of their small home valley, Mike Roberts was saying: "I ain't so good at figures, but it looks to me like we could sell a year from this comin' fall and clear close to two thousand between us."

The gangling Mike rode disjointedly, awkwardly, but Jim had noticed that he could travel that way for a full day and show no sign of tiredness even though he was little more than skin and bones.

"The heck with sellin' next year," Red said. "Between you and me and Ralph, we got close to a hundred full-grown steers right now. If any sellin's to be done, we'll peddle the old stuff." He cast an admiring glance at the bawling yearlings up ahead, now rounding the last pine spur that shut off a view of the valley, of home. "Mighty fine batch of culls Wright sold us."

Jim was about to comment on that when he rounded the last clump of oak brush and looked down across the long green meadow. What he saw made him catch his breath sharply. "Look!" he cried.

Until he pointed, they stared at him as though he'd gone a little off his head. Then they saw it.

Between the new-cut cedar posts of their north fence stretched their six strands of new wire. Only now the wire sagged instead of lining out tightly as it had a week ago. Near each post lay tangled coils of wire, and flanking each side of the creek the grass was trampled down in a wide swath, the unmistakable sign of cattle having been driven through.

Red sobbed a bitter curse and spurred his pony out around the herd and ahead of it. Mike followed. Jim, not wanting to turn the yearlings loose until they were inside the line of the fence, stayed where he was, steadily pushing on the animals. He didn't have to ride down there to look over the damage. It was plain enough at this distance.

When the herd reached the line of the fence, Red came pounding in on Jim. His face was bleached in anger, and his lips were bloodless, tight-pressed.

"Every damned strand cut between every post," he said flatly. "What we can see from here is a hundred dollars gone to hell. Jim, I'm huntin' me some Bar Cross meat to throw some lead at! And it won't be the beef Nugent and Ben Starr drove through here!"

Jim reined in, letting the cattle drift on. Mike came up, his angular frame unwieldy at his pony's racking trot. He shook his head and said gravely: "We couldn't patch it sound enough to hold a litter of kittens."

When Jim remained silent, Red bridled: "Well, what're we waitin' on?"

"I was just thinkin'," Jim drawled deliberately, "that Nugent is probably countin' on our stormin' in there, lookin' for a scrap."

"Let the sidewinder count on it! He's gettin' it!" Red exploded.

"What's better than lettin' some daylight through Nugent? Or Starr? Or maybe both?" Mike demanded.

"Just thinkin' about it sets my hand to itchin' for the feel of a gun," Jim admitted.

"But sure as we started shootin', we'd have our necks stretched before another month was out. No, we got to think of another way."

"Name one," Red said caustically.

"Nugent will say we fenced his critters off from water. He'll. . . ."

"He don't have to bring his stuff through here, does he?" Red asked hotly. "He runs his critters up to hill pasture each spring, then brings 'em down again in the fall. But it wouldn't be much out of his way to swing north a couple miles before he cuts into the hills. Why did he have to come through here? Why couldn't he have told us he was comin'?" Red thought a moment, then added another outburst: "Hang it, I'm talkin' like he had a right to do this!"

"That's what he'll claim," Jim said. "He's driven his stuff through here for years. He can claim prior rights to us. What's more, he'll make it stick."

"Then what do we do?" asked Mike.

"We forget the cut wire and tackle the thing that put it there . . . the new law," Jim told him. "They left the way open for an appeal. We'll make one."

"With about as much chance of changin' it as a caught rabbit has of talkin' a pack o' coyotes out of eatin' him," Red said scornfully. "It's no dice, Jim. Remember what old man

Wright told us about that rulin' the other night after we made the deal with him, when he tried to make his peace with us for havin' voted for this fence law? He said Nugent had enough against every commissioner to push through anything he wanted. You recollect his tellin' about keeping that loggin' outfit away from his timber. Nugent's holdin' that over his head."

Jim nodded. "But I'm also rememberin' how he hates Nugent's guts. So do the others, accordin' to him."

"Sure. But what good does that do us?"

"I don't know yet," Jim answered honestly. "But right now I'm leavin' you two to patch that fence tight enough to hold this herd over-night. I'm headed back to see Wright, to ask a few questions. On the way down tomorrow, I'll stop in town long enough to arrange with Ross and Gant to bring up our appeal at the next commission meetin'. It's set for day after tomorrow."

Red was having a hard time to keep from showing his disgust, much as he liked Jim. Finally he said helplessly: "But the appeal won't get us anywhere."

Jim gave his partner a long, grave look. "Red," he said, "the three of us have gone along together this far, and it's worked pretty well. We've made a good start. Let's don't do anything that'll give Nugent the chance to bust it up for good. Give me two days to prove my way's best. If it don't work, I'll ride with you to the Bar Cross and burn it down, if you want. But give me a chance first."

Red's angry glance dropped. He shrugged. "I can wait."

"How about you, Mike?" Jim asked.

"If you got even half an idea what to do, you're better off than me," was Mike's answer. "I can wait, too."

"Then I'll see you tomorrow." Jim reined the chestnut around and started back up the meadow.

"Now what do you suppose he's cookin' up?" Mike drawled.

Red was a long time giving his answer. As he waited, his anger cooled, and he was remembering a few things about Jim Lance. "No tellin'," he said finally. "But whatever it is, it's liable to be good."

Chapter Six

"Jim Makes Plans"

Jim was back by ten the following morning. When Mike and Red hinted that they'd like to know what he'd talked about with Wright, his answer was evasive.

"Nothin' much," he said. "He was about as careful of what he said as a bank president bein' hit for a loan with no security. But he'll listen to our appeal. Ralph is goin' to do the talkin' for us. We aren't even goin' into town tomorrow."

"Ralph!" Red breathed explosively. "Ralph can't get up there and talk to those highbinders! The first time they say . . . 'No.' . . . he'll give up."

Mike, knowing Ralph Pope even better than Red, said: "That's right, Jim. If we got a prayer of changin' the rulin' Ralph'll spoil it."

Jim shrugged. "Well, they're expectin' me, even if I told Ralph to take my place. I can go in, if we decide it's best. But before then we've got some fence to put up. How much of our wire was cut?"

"They didn't touch the sides, but they sure wore out their cutters at the south end," Red said dismally. "Just the same as what you saw up north yesterday."

"We can do a job if the sides are whole," Jim said. "I had an idea. See what you think of it. We could take two wires off the sides and have enough to string four lengths across the ends. That way, we'd have a good four-wire fence all the way around. Here's what I was thinkin'. If they back down on liftin' that ruling, we can ask 'em to change the legal fence from six to four wires. That way, we'll be able to squeeze through without layin' out any more cash."

Red was quick to say: "Nugent wouldn't let 'em change their law. Why do you think he cut all this wire? So we'd spend ourselves poor buyin' new. Come next fall and he'll do it again. He knows damned well we can't stand that more'n a couple times without goin' broke. If we pick a scrap with him, he'll get that hog-fat law man he elected to arrest us, claimin' he had the right to drive his critters through here. If we don't repair our fences and stretch six wires, he'll have us arrested just the same, claimin' we don't have a legal fence. Jim, I don't see one blasted way out except to go over to the Bar Cross, have our try at Nugent, and then high-tail out o' the country. If we're licked, we can raise plenty trouble before we pull out."

"But they may change their law to make a four-wire fence legal," Jim said.

"With Nugent callin' the turn?" Red said bitterly. "Guess again."

"Maybe Nugent won't be there to call the turn," drawled Jim.

Both Mike's and Red's glance whipped to him. They could read nothing in his expression; it was sober, nothing else.

"You got somethin' in your craw," Red said. "Spill it."

"You gave me till tomorrow," reminded Jim. He went on, ignoring Red's words. "We'll bunch all that cut wire and drag it down here into one batch by the lane where it opens through the south line. It'll be handy to the house, and, when we have some spare time, we can mend it and wind it back on the spools. Someone might want to buy it from us second-hand."

Red, alongside Mike, nudged the taller man who was about to say something. When Mike looked down, Red said to Jim: "I think you're loco. But it's worth a try. Well, when do we start work? Now?"

"Now," Jim agreed.

Red and Mike pulled on their chaps and started out to the corral. When they were out of earshot of the house, Red said to his lanky partner: "Let's just tag along and see what he's workin' on, feller."

Mike was baffled and showed it. "What's he got up his sleeve?"

"Maybe he don't know yet. But it's his money, not ours, in that fence. Unless my sights are out of line, he's not goin' to let Nugent get away with this. And he sure ain't goin' to forget us when it comes to the pay-off. The only thing that worries me is he might go on a lonesome and chouse Nugent. So we got to watch him and not let him buy into trouble on his own."

For the rest of the morning and that afternoon until dark, neither Red nor Mike let Jim out of his sight. There was little talk as they worked the lines of the side fences, taking down two of the strands, coiling them on spools, spacing the remaining four strands with new staples. With a suggestion or two from Jim they developed some teamwork and worked fast. Mike went ahead, prying out staples; Red coiled the extra wire; Jim worked with the block and tackle, quickly stretching each strand in its new place and then going back along it to hammer in the new staples.

Late in the afternoon clouds banked against the higher hills, and, as the early dusk gathered, it began to rain. Red and Mike would have liked to quit rather than get a soaking. But Jim kept doggedly on with the work. Finally, when it was too dark to see, he told them: "We can go back down and eat and come back with lanterns."

"Why all the hurry?" Mike asked. "I'm wore out."

"So am I. But we've got to hold those yearlings in case this storm works up some thunder and lightning, for one thing. For another, I've told Ralph he can tell the commissioners tomorrow that we've already got a tight, four-strand fence built. Wright knows what happened to the other one."

So they ate their meal, left a pot of coffee on the stove, and rode out into the rainy, windswept night, each with a lantern. By nine, the east and west fences were up, and they were at the north end of their section, tearing down the sagging, patched three wires Mike and Red had strung after dark last night. On this shorter fence the work went faster, the only delay being the down-angling stretch where the fence crossed the creek. There they had to anchor the wire to a big boulder in the creek.

They were riding away from the stream when Jim, slightly ahead, suddenly dropped the rope with which he was dragging two spools of wire, put his spurs to his chestnut, and raced off into the darkness. Red shouted after him, then followed. All at once, off ahead and to Red's left, a gun beat hollowly against the murmur of the rain. Close in front of Red, Jim's gun answered in two quick flashes against the pitch darkness. Red drew his gun and reined his pony in the direction of that first shot. He heard a horse pounding in on him, slowed, and nearly collided with Jim.

They went on together, climbing the stiff slope to the timber at the meadow's edge. All at once they were in a thick tangle of scrub oak. Jim called — "Back!" — and led the way down out of the thicket. Then he held up a hand, and they reined their ponies to a stand.

Against the drone of the rain they heard faintly a horse's quick-striking hooffalls going away higher in the timber.

When Red lifted his reins, waiting for the word to go ahead, Jim drawled: "Let him go. He can tell Nugent what we're doin'."

"Why not chase him down?"

"You can't even see your horse's ears, it's so dark. We wouldn't stand a chance of catchin' him. Besides, I want Nugent to know what we're up to. It'll worry him."

They started back down to the creek. They had gone but a few rods when Red said in edgy sarcasm: "Any time you want to let us in on this, Mike and me are willin' to listen, friend."

"All right, you can have it now," Jim said. "We finish the south fence tomorrow mornin'. Around noon you and me and Mike head out of here, toward Nugent's. Then. . . ."

He was still explaining the details to Red when they rode down to Mike. He had to begin all over again for the tall man's benefit.

"How does it sound?" he asked, when he had finished. "Too far-fetched?"

"Plenty," Red said. Then he added, his drawl tinged with excitement: "But it's a chance, even if it is a long one. Man, wouldn't that burn Nugent up if we can swing it!"

"*If* we can," Mike said skeptically. Then, when Red's glance swung sharply at him: "It ain't that I'm not with you. But I'm wonderin' about Ralph. He's liable to get tongue-tied in front of those jaspers. Remember, he works for Ross. It'd be just like him to worry more about takin' the time from his job than about what you told him to do."

"He'll hold up his end," Jim said. He hoped he sounded more sure of Ralph than he felt.

Chapter Seven

"Nugent Rides His Luck"

The next day was cold, with low clouds hiding the sun and an occasional spitting of rain. Ed Nugent ate his noon meal early and directly afterward called down to Ben Starr to have one of the crew saddle his black.

He spent some minutes in his bedroom, cleaning and oiling a short-barreled .38, that he finally thrust into a clip holster strapped to his chest below his left armpit. He was wearing a gun on his hip, but, remembering what Ben had had to say about Jim Lance's way of handling a gun, he was taking this added precaution.

He was a man who never took chances, never gave an enemy the advantage. Although he had no thought of how he might use this second gun, or that he'd need it at all, he was being careful. He even changed from the coat he was in the habit of wearing and put on a canvas jacket he used mostly for hunting. It fit loosely and, even when buckled down the front, wasn't tight enough to show the bulge of the gun in the clip holster. His last thought as he pulled on a poncho was that he must remember to keep the jacket buckled so it wouldn't fall open and expose the .38.

Down at the bunkhouse, he stopped at the door long enough to call in: "Ben, I've changed my mind. You'd better come to town with me."

Starr appeared shortly and joined him, and they went down to the corral together. It took the ramrod an extra three minutes to rope a horse and saddle, and Nugent was impatient at the delay, for it had started raining again, and the spirited black wanted to go.

Finally they started out the trail leading to the town road. As they struck the road and swung into it, Nugent asked abruptly: "You're sure about what you saw last night? They were stetchin' only four wires?"

"Didn't I check that side fence on the way back?" Starr said.

Nugent rode on in silence for another quarter mile. Then, as abruptly as before, he asked: "What's their play?"

"Don't ask me, boss. It might be they. . . ." Suddenly Starr straightened in the saddle, looking ahead and to the left of the trail. "Ain't that them now?" he asked quickly. "That's sure Roberts's big bay." He lifted a hand to point, then swore. "They just went into them trees across there."

"Where?" Nugent asked sharply, for the direction in which Starr pointed was Bar Cross range. "How many were there?"

"Three. Don't Lance ride a chestnut with white front stockings?" When Nugent nodded, the foreman said: "Then that was him! What do you reckon they're doin' off there? Didn't you say Lance was to be at the meetin' this afternoon?"

With a curt nod, Nugent reined off the road and down across an open stretch toward the trees Starr had indicated. The rain had let up, but the clouds seemed to be dissolving toward the soaked ground, laying down a thin fog that obscured the distance. Nugent hurried, wanting a look at the riders Ben had seen. The black, under the touch of spurs, lined out at a fast run.

Nugent rounded the neck of timber in time to see the three riders topping the crest of an adjoining rise some two hundred yards away. He recognized at once Mike Roberts's tall shape and was almost sure that it was Lance astride the chestnut.

Pulling in, Nugent waited for Starr to come up. When his foreman was alongside, he snapped: "Get back to the lay-out! Get every man you can, give him a rifle, and cover the place. Put a couple in the house, one in the barn, and have the rest fort up on that hill behind the corrals. They're to stay down and out of sight. Now beat it!"

"What's up, boss?"

"Don't know yet. But Lance could've trumped up that story of comin' to the meetin' to catch us off guard. It'd be a sweet chance for him to burn us out, knowin' you'd be with me in town. Hurry it, Ben! I'm stickin' with 'em to see where they go."

Starr jerked his horse around, raked his sharp spurs along the animal's flanks, and bent low in the saddle as he went away at a hard run. Nugent stared narrowly toward the hill crest where the three riders had disappeared, his glance wary, his mind groping for a further explanation of what he had seen. He had the uneasy feeling that he should have laced a rifle on his saddle before setting out for town. The thought made him laugh grimly. How could he have known he was running into this kind of trouble?

Instead of going directly on over the hill the way Lance and his two companions had, Nugent swung off to the left, following the line of trees. He rode at a fast trot, right hand through the pocket slit of his poncho and gripping his Colt.

From a higher point on the hill crest, he had a glimpse of the three homesteaders, crossing a grassy pocket a quarter mile ahead. They were narrowing a circle that would bring them into the Bar Cross from the west, where timber ran down close to the outbuildings.

Nugent smiled thinly as he put the black down the slope, angling a little so as to make up the distance they had gained on him. If his guess was right, if Lance, Curtis, and Roberts had hoped to toll him into town so as to even the score for their cut wire, then they were due for a surprise. Thinking of the trap he had sent Ben Starr to set, his smile broadened. Maybe, just maybe, everything would be settled before the afternoon was over. "Better yet," he said aloud, "I'm in the clear if we cut all three of 'em down. They come here askin' for trouble, and they got it!"

During the next forty minutes, he glimpsed his quarry three more times. They were taking their time. But, instead of riding in on the Bar Cross, they had struck out in a line angling south and away from it. Nugent grew puzzled, less certain that he had guessed their plans. They seemed to be riding aimlessly. Once, as he closed in and got a nearer look at them, he saw Curtis swing away from the others and ride out toward a bunch of steers, grazing in a grassy pocket of the timber. The redhead circled the steers, then cut back to his two companions.

"What in Tophet are they doin'?" Nugent muttered.

All at once he remembered the time and took out his watch. It was a quarter to two! The time of the meeting had been set for two. Even if he killed the black, he couldn't hope to get to town now in time for the meeting.

Abruptly Nugent was laughing at himself. What did it matter now that he was missing the meeting? The only reason he had been going was because of the note Wright had sent out this morning warning him that Lance was going to appeal the new fence law. Well, here was Lance in sight a quarter of a mile away. So long as Lance wasn't in Rimrock to put in his appeal, any other business that might come up could be forgotten. There wouldn't be anything important; there hardly ever was at these regular meetings.

So, far more out of curiosity than for any other reason, Nugent followed the three homesteaders. Once more he saw Red Curtis ride out to look over a bunch of grazing steers. Then, half an hour after he'd looked at his watch, he saw the three men ride down a slope, hit the town road, and take it in an easy lope.

He was sore now, sore at himself for having wasted most of an afternoon riding in the cold and rain, sore at Lance and Curtis and Roberts for not having fallen into his trap. Why hadn't Lance gone into town to appear before the commissioners? The more Nugent thought about it, the more it worried him. There was one logical answer. After deciding to make the appeal, Lance had changed his mind, realizing the futility of getting the fence law changed. But was this answer the right one? And why had the three homesteaders taken that long and apparently aimless ride this afternoon?

When he came to the side trail that led off to his lay-out, Nugent stopped. Half a mile ahead along the road he could see the trio he had been following for the past two hours jogging on in toward town. Why bother going into Rimrock himself? It was five miles in and five back, and he had no business now to take him. But that nagging small devil of curiosity was still in him. In the end he rode on past the Bar Cross trail branching and down the town road.

It was after four when Nugent swung in off Rimrock's street to the tie rail in front of the bank. He was looping his reins over the pole when Harvey Wright came down the walk, spotted him, and came over.

"What happened to you, Ed?" asked Wright.

"Got tied up on something out at the house," Nugent said. "Anything come up at the meetin' I should know about?"

"Nothin' much," was the older man's reply. "Harkness was there with the hide of a beef he found butchered out at the north end of his place. As usual, he's tryin' to start another Indian war. Claims those Utes up north sneaked off the reservation and helped themselves to meat with his brand on it."

"He knew they'd do that when he moved up into that forsaken hole, didn't he?"

"That's what we reminded him," Wright said. "By the way, Ralph Pope turned up with a story about you takin' a herd through his place and leavin' a lot of cut wire behind. More cut wire than you had to."

Nugent was irritated by Wright's narrow stare. "What if I did? Haven't I been drivin' through that valley for seven years to get my stuff up into the hills?"

Wright nodded. "That's what we reminded Pope. We warned him that by next fall him and his partners would have to put enough big gates on each end of their fence and let you get your stuff through. He claimed that was agreeable to him, and he'd see it done. But. . . ."

When the rancher hesitated, Nugent asked sharply: "But what?"

65

"Well, it was this way. Pope said his partners had used up most of the their ready cash buyin' that wire. It'd about break 'em to lay out money for more. He asked if we'd change that new fence law to make a four-strand fence do instead of a six."

Nugent's face colored. His big hands knotted as he saw what was coming. "Don't tell me you double-crossed me on that?" he breathed.

Wright's face showed hurt and amazement. "Double-crossed? How would that be double-crossing' you? The state says a single wire is a legal fence. We say six on any piece under one section. Man, you still got your law. What's the difference between four wires and six when it comes to a fence bein' solid? That's all you want, ain't it?"

Nugent's fury was all-consuming. For a moment he couldn't speak. When he did, he snarled: "They asked for it! Now they'll get it! They. . . ."

"Careful, Ed," Wright cut in. "Lance might hear you."

Nugent turned. Thirty feet away, turning in toward Nugent and Wright, came Lance, Roberts, and Curtis.

Nugent glared at them as they approached. However, they didn't seem to notice. Red Curtis reined in close by and said politely:

"Ed, some of those critters I turned loose last fall have strayed down to your end of the flats. Mind if we come across and gather 'em one of these days?"

Here, Nugent realized, was the reason the three homesteaders had been riding the Bar Cross range this afternoon. He was apoplectic. By wasting his time following these three he had missed the chance to block the change in the fence law. He was furious but saw the need for being cautious.

"No objection," he said, trying hard to control his voice. Then he made a mistake, adding: "You sure sneaked that change in the ruling through in nice shape."

The three homesteaders frowned in mock surprise. Jim looked down at Wright. "Change?" he asked blandly. "We decided not to bother even comin' in."

"Pope was there," Wright told Lance. "We heard what he had to say and decided to let it go this time if you strung four good wires."

"That's mighty white of you," Jim drawled. His glance shifted to Nugent. "What do you mean . . . sneaked it through? You were there to bellyache if you didn't like it. Why didn't you argue Ralph down?"

Nugent's lips made a thin line. "You know damned well I wasn't there!" Only now did he see the whole picture and realize that these three had intended he do exactly as he had done this afternoon, follow them and miss the meeting.

Jim looked back as he glanced at his partners, then at Wright again. "What's eatin' him?" he asked. Then he shrugged, said to the others — "Let's be movin', boys." — and led the way on up the street.

"I won't forget this, Wright," Nugent growled.

But he got little satisfaction from the old rancher, who looked as innocent as the homesteaders. "You better get some liver medicine, Ed. No one's done a thing to you that I know of. As for changin' that rulin', I gave you warnin' they were goin' to appeal it. Now you give me the devil because you weren't even interested enough to come in to the meetin'." His glance was steady on Nugent, guileless, questioning.

At that moment, Ed Nugent first suspected that Harvey Wright might have been in with the homesteaders on this deception. But he wasn't sure. Still being cautious, he decided to wait for further proof. Suddenly he had an idea. He smiled easily and said: "Forget it, Wright. Guess maybe I've stuck my neck out too far on this thing. So would you if you'd made the kind of a start I did with Lance."

"He ain't so bad to get on with, Ed. All him

or his partners are after is to be let alone. Try it once and you'll be surprised how little they'll bother you."

Nugent nodded. "That's about all there's left for me to do. But understand," he added ominously, "if they step out o' line, I'm goin' after 'em."

"Sure," the older man said, almost genially. "I'd go after 'em, too. But they'll keep in line. I'd be willing to bet on it."

"You'd better be right." Nugent kept his face serious. To add more conviction to his apparent change of mind, he said: "I've been so busy with this mess lately I've been lettin' my work go. It'll do me good to forget it and start ranchin' again."

Wright eyed him closely. "You sound like you mean it."

"I do. I'm sick of the whole thing. If those *hombres* keep out of my way, I reckon I can get on with them."

"That's the way to talk." Wright took out his watch and looked at it, abruptly frowning. "Say, I'll have to be goin'. That cook of mine has got me so buffaloed I'm scared to be late for a meal. Be seein' you, Ed."

Nugent watched the old rancher go up the walk, glowering after him, wondering whether or not his suspicions of several minutes ago had any basis of fact. Talking to

Wright back there, he'd suddenly seen the possibility that the man had actually helped the homesteaders put through the change in the fence law. Things had gone off too smoothly not to have been planned beforehand. Ralph Pope was a shy, retiring man, too ineffectual to have persuaded men like Wright, Ross, and Gant on changing the ruling without some help. Had Wright, then, helped Pope argue the other two into making the change? Had Wright known that he, Nugent, wouldn't be there to protest against the change?

Because he saw that possibility, Nugent had quickly altered his outward attitude toward the homesteaders in his talk with Wright. He'd had a purpose in doing it, and now he wondered if he'd been convincing enough so that it would net him anything.

Reining his horse around, he rode back out the street as the premature dusk began to settle out of a leaden sky. He knew what he was going to do but wasn't at all sure that it would work out. Harvey Wright was nobody's fool. If he'd had a hand in this, he'd be careful not to expose it.

As Nugent cut off the main trail and headed into the hills, he had little hope that he was on the way to discovering anything. But the outcome of the afternoon, the ease with which the homesteaders had deceived him, galled so deeply that he was willing to go to any lengths for his revenge. What he was doing now was acting on a far-fetched impulse. It might not work out, but, so long as there was even a slight chance, he was stubborn enough to follow that chance up.

Thirty minutes after leaving town, Ed Nugent was tying his reins to the top wire of the homesteaders' east fence. It was pitch dark now. Down a ways the light from the window of Ford's shack made an orange pinpoint against the blackness. Nugent climbed the fence and walked down through the dripping trees, his boots slurring over the thick carpeting of rain-softened pine needles. Closer, he caught the smell of cooking meat and was abruptly hungry and wishing he was home. Thinking of the time, and the slim hunch he was playing, he almost stopped and turned back.

But finally he went on, and in a few minutes he was too absorbed in the immediate problem of soundlessly approaching the homesteaders' shack to think of his doubts.

As far as he knew, there was no dog on the place. But, on the chance that there might be, he picked up a wrist-thick stick he stumbled upon and carried it as a club. The window to the shack gradually took shape as he rounded

71

the back of the barn. He took off his poncho and dropped it there, afraid that it might rub against something and give him away. Seeing a man's shape move across the light inside the room, he went slower, putting each foot down carefully before he eased his weight onto it.

He was halfway across the back yard when a horse out front whickered and pawed the ground. He stopped in his tracks, considering this. The three homesteaders would undoubtedly have turned their horses into the corral or meadow. Then what was a horse doing out front?

When Nugent guessed the answer, his pulse jumped to a quicker beat. All his misgivings left him. Recklessly he walked straight in on the cabin, hugged the wall, and edged in toward the window.

Abruptly the deep undertone of a voice sounded out to him. His fists knotted, and he breathed shallowly as he recognized that voice as belonging to Harvey Wright. Two more steps put him close enough to the ill-fitted window frame to let him distinguish the rancher's words.

". . . didn't sound to me like he meant it. What's your idea, Lance?"

"The same as it's been since the mornin' I first ran into him. He won't quit till he's run us out . . . or until we can show him it's easier to let us alone than to keep after us."

Red's laugh echoed in the room beyond the wall. "He sure looked mad enough to bite a horseshoe in two there on the street. Did he wise up to how you'd helped us, Wright?"

"No, I don't think so," the rancher answered. "But we've got to be careful."

"Just why are you doin' this for us?" asked Lance.

"Because I hate a range hog," came the rancher's quick and testy answer. "A range hog roots up and swallows everything around him, same as any other hog. Give him enough to feed on, and he eats that and hunts more. He'll eat till he's gorged, lie around a bit, and then pack his guts again. Don't you boys get it in your heads I'm doin' you any favor! I'm doin' myself the favor. If Nugent runs you off and takes over this valley, next year he'll be pushin' the man on the other side of him out. That jasper's got an appetite for power that'd tie a hog's for corn. He'll grow fat the same as a hog, but fat on power. He's already talked us into electin' a sheriff we knew was worthless. Why? So he could get a favor done if he ever wanted one. He blackmailed us into passin' that fence law. He'll crowd us into other things until we're as crooked as he is. Uhn-huh, it's not you I'm doin' this for, it's myself. I'm stoppin' Nugent before he gets big enough to tell me what to do and make me like it."

Nugent listened and had a hard time stifling a laugh. The old fool sounded pretty convincing. He was making these saddle bums believe him.

This was all Nugent wanted to know. Stepping well back out of the light, he headed for the barn. There, pulling on his slicker again, he seriously tried to think how he could catch Wright on the way out tonight, shoot him, and frame the killing on the homesteaders. But, no, he could wait for his revenge on the rancher. First he was settling things with Lance and the other two. And he knew how he was going to do it.

At the Bar Cross less than forty minutes afterward, Nugent was sitting down to a heaping plate of food kept warm for him by the cook. As he started eating, he sent the cook down to the bunkhouse for Ben Starr.

The foreman came hurrying up, full of questions. What had happened this afternoon? What had scared the homesteaders off? Where had Nugent been all this time?

Nugent answered all this. Then, as he wolfed his meal, he began telling Ben Starr something that made the Bar Cross ramrod sit straighter in his chair and listen without interrupting.

Chapter Eight

"An Offer"

Six days after they had led Nugent on that aimless ride over Bar Cross range, Red and Jim were dragging the broken lengths of their cut wire into a twisted pile outside their south fence and to one side of the gate to the lane that led to the shack. They had accomplished much since that night of Wright's visit. Their hundred yearlings had been branded; they had dragged down pine logs and built two big gates in their fence, one near the creek at the upper north line, another here at the south end. Even the lane was now fenced with four strands of tight wire. Tomorrow, they planned on going to Rimrock to buy a second-hand plow and some oat and alfalfa seed. They had already staked out ten acres near the creek that was to become their alfalfa strip.

But these last few days had given all three of them a feeling of uneasiness. Red worded it now as he threw a coil of tangled wire to the top of the springy mound, pulled off a thick leather glove, and looked across at Jim. "What do you reckon's happened to Nugent?"

Jim shrugged. "No tellin'."

"Y'know damned well he's up to somethin'."

"Maybe," drawled Jim.

"What you mean, maybe?"

"Just maybe."

Red shook his head. Sometimes Jim was as close-mouthed as an Apache, the redhead was thinking. He pulled on his glove again and was about to reach for another long, twisted length of wire when he happened to look down the trail to see a rider coming in along it. A moment later he recognized Ben Starr and said quickly: "Heads up!"

Starr drew rein only a few feet out from Jim and sat the saddle of his chunky bay, looking down a moment at the mound of wire. A slow, almost good-natured grin came to his coarse face.

"It's a shame the boss didn't change his mind before we did that," he said. "Could've saved you some work, eh?"

"How's he changed his mind?" Red queried, after waiting a moment for Jim to speak and Jim's remaining silent.

Starr shrugged. "Don't ask me. Only whenever I mention you gents, he says something like . . . 'Let 'em go,' . . . or . . . 'We got enough to do without botherin' about them.' I figured he was sick. Now he sends me over here wantin' me to ask you, real polite, if you're open to a deal."

Red snorted. "The answer's no!"

As Starr's face took on an angry look, Jim said: "We're listenin'. What kind of a deal?"

"Well, there's a catch to it," Starr admitted frankly. "The boss remembered how you was across a few days ago lookin' for those critters of Red's and Mike's strayin' around down on the flats. He wants to know if you're gatherin' 'em soon to push up above?"

Jim glanced at Red. Only yesterday they had talked about this and decided that they would have to forget this long and tedious job until fall or maybe even until next spring. Together, Red and Mike owned close to seventy head of cattle that they had turned onto free range over the past two or three years, letting the animals shift for themselves. Although their number wasn't great, they were scattered over a vast, open range and rounding them up would take time that might be better spent working on the place. So it had been decided that, unless the partners needed money in a hurry, they'd let the cattle go another year.

Red understood Jim's glance and looked at

Starr. "What if we do figure to go after 'em?" he asked belligerently.

Starr gave a slow shake of the head. "You sure are feelin' salty, brother," he said mildly, in a way that didn't quite fit him. "Here I come, tryin' to do you a favor, and all I get is back talk."

Jim cut in before Red had a chance to answer that. "We'd figured to forget those critters until next spring. But what's your proposition?"

"Ed's havin' some of the same trouble," Starr said. "Every year we lose a hundred or more head o' beef that stray south. The outfits down that way ain't particular about savin' our stuff for us. The last two years we've sent a rep down for Soldad beef and all he brought back was what he gathered himself. So the boss has decided to send the whole crew down there and work over that country to see what kind of a gather he can make. They left four days ago."

"What's that got to do with us?" asked Jim.

"Wait'll I finish," the Bar Cross man said. "When the boys work up as far as our range with what stuff they pick up, Ed wants 'em to drag the flats for any other Bar Cross critters we might've missed a few weeks ago before we took our herd up above. Now if you gents want, we'll gather your beef at the same time, cut it out, and turn it over to you. Only in return for the favor, you've got to help us with the gather for a couple of days. Probably won't take more'n three days at the outside and you'll have the job finished and all your critters rounded up to put where you want. You'll have some calf brandin' you can get off your hands, too, if you want."

On the face of it, Starr's offer made sense. Jim could tell by Red's look that his partner realized this. Nugent was offering to save them some hard work, and, the way Starr explained it, they would be doing a much more thorough job than they could do on their own. Still, it wasn't like Ed Nugent to be doing this favor. *Unless,* Jim thought, *he really meant what he said the other day about tryin' to get on with us.*

"What's the catch, Starr?" Red asked querulously.

"Confound it, can't you give Ed a break?" Starr replied sourly. "He's tryin' to make up for what he figures was a mistake. Give him a chance. You'll be helpin' him now when he needs it. He'll be helpin' you. What's the catch to that?"

Jim thought he saw what it was and said: "Why is Nugent makin' a gather at this time of year? Fall's the time for that."

"There's a reason," admitted Starr. "The

boss heard from a friend of his down near Deming who's buyin' heavy to stock a place back in Kansas so he can hit the fall market at the right time. He'll take a couple of hundred head from us right now at good prices. So, instead of goin' above for the critters, Ed figures he'll do two jobs at once. Only we need some extra hands to help at this end."

Jim felt Red's glance on him, and, when he looked around, he saw Red's hesitant eagerness. His partner was plainly leaving it up to him to decide. Thinking back over what Starr had said, Jim could see no loopholes in it. Nugent was evidently needing help and doing a favor in return for one. On the surface, at least, he was offering to let bygones be bygones.

"When do you want us?" Jim asked Starr.

"Tomorrow. The three of you get started around noon and head for our 'Dobe Springs camp. By the middle of the afternoon, the crew should have worked that far and you can pitch right in with 'em. I won't be there." Starr smiled ruefully and held up his right hand. "The way you busted up this mitt, I'm no good with a rope or anything else much. So I'm doin' odd jobs on the place for a while."

"Wish there could have been some way of gettin' around that," Jim drawled.

Starr shrugged. "Well, I've forgotten it.

80

You better, too." He turned his pony back down the trail. "Be seein' you," he called, and lifted a hand as he went away.

They watched him in silence until he was nearly out of sight. Finally Red said: "This is the break we been lookin' for. If Nugent eases off, we're set."

Jim was trying to peg something that hadn't been quite right about Ben Starr's story. Finally he thought he had it. "He made sense until he mentioned his hand. But that was layin' it on pretty thick. It's not like Starr to forget so easy."

Red looked around sharply at him. "What're you tryin' to tell me?"

"That we'd better be careful."

The redhead frowned, not understanding, and Jim went on: "Suppose Nugent wants to toll us away from the place so he can come in here and wreck it, burn it down, do anything he wants?"

"He couldn't get away with it. Even with his bought law, Wright and a few others would climb all over him for a thing like that."

Jim shrugged, thought a moment. "We'll give it a try," he said finally. "Only I don't like it."

"Want me to catch Starr and tell him it's no deal?"

"No," Jim said. "We'll go out there tomorrow and see what happens."

81

Chapter Nine

"Bar Cross Double-Cross"

Ed Nugent's 'Dobe Springs camp had once been a stage station. But in the ten years since the new Rimrock-Whitefield road had ignored it by some eight miles, it had been abandoned. Two years ago Nugent, seeing the possibilities of the camp, had bought it. Not only was it used by Nugent, but by other ranchers at this south end of the county as well. Twice a year, early in the spring at calving time and in the fall at roundup, several outfits based their crews here.

The big circular corral had been enlarged to hold upward of two hundred animals. Nugent had thrown a fan-shaped earth dam below the spring that, in the old days, had been needed only to keep the log troughs full before running down a nearby wash. Now a half-acre pond lay below the spring.

At three that afternoon, Jim, Mike, and Red watered their ponies and their heavily loaded pack animal at that pond, Jim meanwhile looking across the shallow depression to the towering cottonwoods and the crumbling weather-washed adobe walls of what had once been the main building. It sprawled under the trees, roofless, a skeletal reminder of better days. The log *vigas* that had supported its roof now formed the back wall of a long, ugly bunkhouse closer to the corral and out from the trees. Because this spot was fairly remote from the hills, all but that back log wall of the bunkhouse was built of an odd assortment of materials, the gray, weathered boards of one of the station's original sheds, patches of warped and peeling pine slab, even some tar paper across one end. The shake roof was badly in need of repair; some of the split cedar had been loosened by the high winds of early spring to leave gaping holes. But each spring and fall the building offered comparatively luxurious quarters for upward of twenty men, and it was good enough to serve its purpose.

All the way across here, Jim's restless glance had studied the distance to the south and west, trying to spot Bar Cross' crew and the herd of strays that was being brought in. But he had picked up no dust sign all the way to the blued horizon of the flats. It was worrying him.

He lifted his chestnut's head from the water before the animal was through drinking, said shortly — "Goin' up to have a look." — and rode up the nearest rise and out of the shallow bowl in which the pond lay.

Mike looked after him and, when he was out of hearing, said to Red: "He's as jumpy as a cat."

Red nodded. "What if they are late? I'd rather loaf the rest of the day than work anyway."

Still, Jim's restlessness became contagious later when they had gone across to the corral, off saddled, and carried their bedrolls into the bunkroom. They spent a good half hour working, sweeping out the torn fragments of a blanket and some newspapers the pack rats had chewed, dragging in dead cedar and cottonwood for the night's fire, filling the water barrel. When the jobs were done, Jim again walked up out of the depression to take another look out across the flats.

When he came back, his face bore a worried frown. "I don't like this," he said.

"Suppose they had better luck than they'd counted on?" Mike asked. "A powerful lot o' Soldad steers have strayed down over the county line these last two years. Quit worryin'. If they don't show up tonight, they'll be along tomorrow."

Jim nodded and seemed to agree. The time dragged until supper. Mike, acting as cook, made an elaborate ceremony of preparing the meal, emptying a big can of tomatoes into a jerky stew, making baking-powder biscuits in a Dutch oven, and brewing a big pot of coffee. They took their time about eating, except for Jim, who wolfed his food and walked off into the gathering darkness before the other two were half finished.

This time he was gone for quite a while, better than twenty minutes. When he did walk back into the light of the fire in front of the bunkshack, Red and Mike were both startled, so soundlessly did he appear.

What he said jerked them from their lazy contentment. It was: "You two can stick it out here if you want. But I'm headed back."

"Now?" Red asked, pushing up from where he had lying, head pillowed on his saddle. "Jehoshaphat, it'll take us two hours to get home. I've been countin' on a lot o' shut-eye tonight."

"Figure it out for yourself," Jim said slowly. "It's clear tonight. A man could spot the glow of a fire ten miles away. Get up there and have a look for yourself. If Nugent's crew is camped anywhere within ten miles, I've gone blind."

Red stood up now. Mike did, too. They looked at each other, then at Jim.

"What could it add up to?" Mike asked finally.

"Red said yesterday that Nugent wouldn't dare touch the place while we're away. I say he would. If he's tolled us out here so we won't be in his way, the sooner we get back, the better."

Mike, at least, was now thoroughly alarmed. He stepped across to empty the coffee pot into the fire. He looked at his Dutch oven, then at the tarp that lay close by; they had used it in packing the extra horse.

"Why don't we forget this stuff and leave it here till we can get back after it?" he suggested. "We can turn that extra jughead loose. He'll follow us home."

"It'll sure make suckers of us if we get back there and find nothin' wrong," Red said glumly. "Ought to make Ben Starr sore as hell if he's countin' on us to help him here tomorrow."

"Why don't you do like I said, let me go across alone?" Jim said. "If nothing's wrong, I can be back by midnight."

"And supposin' you run into trouble?" Red countered. "No sale, friend. We're sidin' you. Then we can all be back before mornin' if we want."

Ten minutes later they rode out of the shallow bowl in which the cottonwoods made their heavy shadow. They went away fast. Their fire burned brightly for a time. Then,

86

gradually, its blaze died and there was nothing but the red glow of the coals slowly crumbling to a clean white ash.

The shadows had crept in almost to that bed of ashes when a man's heavy-bodied shape came up out of the darkness. He lugged a metal five-gallon can. For a moment he stood barely outside the feeble glow of the fire, looking about him, listening. Gradually the clean woodsmoke smell of the air was tainted with another odor, the pungent smell of coal oil.

Presently Ben Starr strode across to the 'Dobe Springs shack. Inside, he uncorked the can and liberally sprinkled its contents along the floor at the base of the walls. When it was empty, he took out a heavy-bladed jackknife and punched many holes in the sides of the can. He walked down to the pond and threw the can as far out into it as he could. Then he sauntered back to the fire and squatted there, rolling a smoke and lighting it from the glowing end of a small branch.

He looked at his watch and muttered. "Better give 'em another half hour even if they are in a hurry."

It was a trifle longer than that before he went into the cabin, lit a match, and tossed it into a puddle of coal oil.

Chapter Ten

"Fire Tells Its Own Story"

When Ed Nugent saw the sky out across the flats begin to take on a rosy glow, he went down to the bunkhouse, stepped quickly in the door to keep the light from showing, and told his four crewmen playing penny-ante stud at the center table: "Everything's set. Ben's touched it off." He looked to the two windows, making sure that the double blankets hanging over them were nailed tight. Then he gave his orders crisply. "I'll fire the first man that shows a light outside. Stay in here out of sight until you're needed. Where did you put the horses, Kell?"

"Up in the timber," one of the men answered. "Won't take three minutes to get to 'em."

Nugent nodded his approval. With a brusque — "It ought to be in about two hours." — he went out the door and down to the corral, where he saddled a horse and took the road to town, riding fast.

It was a few minutes short of ten when he

pounded down Rimrock's street and slid his pony to a stop in front of the Hillside. Against the lighted window of the saloon he made out several figures.

"Where's the sheriff?" he called sharply.

"In here" — one of the men on the walk replied, adding dryly — "drunk."

Checking a rise in irritation, Nugent jumped from the saddle, tossed his reins over the rail, and hurried in through the Hillside's swing doors.

He saw Ashworth bellied up to the bar, Stetson pushed onto the back of his head, his eyes heavy-lidded and bloodshot. He started toward the law man, feeling the glances of the room's occupants upon him. Evidently they had heard him hail the men out front.

There were, he saw, eight men strung out along the bar, two playing pool at the table up in front with half a dozen watchers standing idly by. Farther back, two poker lay-outs were going, the glare of the lamps hanging over them blue with tobacco smoke. Excitement hit Nugent when he saw that Harvey Wright was one of the players at the back table. He'd hardly dared hope for such luck, even though he had known that the rancher was to be in town overnight to meet a relative arriving on the early stage in the morning.

One mistake Nugent knew he'd made was

in counting on Ashworth. He should have remembered the man's liking for liquor and sent in word that he was to go easy on the bottle tonight.

He stepped in alongside the sheriff. "Hank, a fire's blazin' out across the flats," he said in a curt, hard voice. "Looks like it could be my 'Dobe Springs camp."

"Huh?" Ashworth grunted, and stared at Nugent blankly out of slitted eyes.

Nugent caught the barkeeper's shake of the head and turned away from the counter to face the men in the room, disgust showing on his face. Those who had been on the walk had followed him in, evidently knowing that his errand was urgent from the way he had run his horse down the street.

"Twenty minutes ago Ben Starr spotted a blaze out across the flats," he announced loudly. "It looks like my camp at 'Dobe Springs. I sent Ben on ahead and came in for help. Who's goin' to ride out there with me?"

"What good'll it do us to go out now," someone asked. "If it was a fire, it's burned down by now."

"Here's the good it'll do us," Nugent answered. "Yesterday I hired those homesteaders above my place to go out and help my crew work that country for strays." His glance settled on Harvey Wright. "Harvey, I told you the other day I'd sent the boys down south to comb that country. Well, I thought to give Lance and Red and Mike a few days' work. They were to meet my outfit at the 'Dobe Springs camp this afternoon. Instead, I got word that the crew had been held up and wouldn't hit the springs until late tomorrow. So that fire looks mighty queer."

"What's queer about a fire?" Wright asked mildly. "Accidents can happen."

"I'll admit that. But there hasn't been any wind tonight. And those three know how to look after a fire. They could put one out before it got a good start. There's plenty of water handy at the springs."

"Then you're accusin' your neighbors of firin' your camp?" Wright asked. His narrowed face had tightened in anger he didn't want to show.

"No, not until I've had my look," Nugent said reasonably. "Starr can tell you I went out of my way to make my peace with those three. I even offered to gather up those steers of Red's and Mike's to save them a job. Now I want witnesses in case this turns out to be what I think it is."

All eyes in the room went to Harvey Wright. Nugent waited for the man to speak, knowing what weight his word bore with the townspeople. Wright hesitated only a moment before coming up out of his chair. "I'll go with you," he said.

The Hillside emptied quickly, and, by the time Nugent had gone to the livery barn and saddled a fresh horse, fourteen men who had scented trouble were ready to hit the old trail out to 'Dobe Springs. Even Henry Ashworth was there, somewhat more sober than he had been back at the bar.

Before he led them out the street, Nugent said: "I want you men to remember this. There wasn't a Bar Cross man within miles of the springs today. Ben and I and the cook were alone at the place. Around noon, all three of us saw Lance, Red Curtis, and Mike Roberts headed out onto the flats. So whatever's happened out there looks like their fault."

"Let's go see what happened before we begin callin' any names, Ed," drawled Wright.

"I'll be the last to call names," Nugent said. He was impressive at that moment, a big, handsome man sitting on a big horse, outwardly trying to be fair toward his enemies. What he said made an impression on his listeners, many of whom held him in awe.

When they ran their horses out the street, not a man among them, with the exception of Harvey Wright, felt anything but sincere sympathy toward Ed Nugent. Wright, for that matter, was himself feeling a little sorry for Nugent. He'd kept his ear to the ground since the last commissioners' meeting, and, according to all reports, Nugent was letting his neighbors strictly alone. Wright was now worried for fear the homesteaders, Red most likely might have taken things in their own hands, not trusting Nugent's seeming change of heart. And if Red had fired the 'Dobe Springs camp, on the theory that he would pay the Bar Cross back for cutting his fence, he had made a bad mistake. Sympathies that had been with the homesteaders would just as quickly turn to Nugent.

It was the thought of Jim Lance that finally calmed Wright and assured him that his worry was groundless. The rancher had learned to respect this newcomer from Texas as he respected few men, and he now reasoned that Jim would never make a mistake like this or let his partners make one. Still, Red Curtis had a fiery temper; he might have gone ahead on his own, without letting Jim know what he was doing.

When Wright followed the others over the rise immediately beyond the cottonwoods at the springs and followed them down toward the big pond, his easing worry mounted again instantly at the ruin he saw. All that remained of the big Bar Cross bunkshack was a heap of glowing embers pluming a billowing cloud of gray smoke into the night sky. The logs that had formed the back wall made a fiery red mound, not quite burned out. The air was tainted with the acrid yet sweetish smell of burning tar paper.

Down below a man walked out of the shadows beyond the shack, and Wright recognized Ben Starr. He rode down with the others to crowd around the Bar Cross foreman, who was saying as he came up: ". . . about gone when I got here."

"Any sign, Ben?" Nugent asked tonelessly.

Starr nodded. "Plenty. They were here. They cooked their supper at a fire in front of the shack and then left. You can still smell the stink of coal oil out front there. They must've slopped some out of whatever they carried it in. Boss, I told you we was wrong trustin' them jaspers!"

"Take it easy, Ben," Nugent said calmly. "We aren't sure yet they did it. Let's try to find some proof."

Starr turned away, grumbling.

"Better light and spread out and look for sign," Nugent told the others. "A couple of you can cut some brush and make a fire out here so we'll have a light. Anyone think to bring a lantern? I didn't."

Two men spoke up, and, shortly, they were

circling down toward the pond, each with a companion, studying the ground for sign. Ben Starr followed after them, calling their attention to the boot tracks he had already spotted. Harvey Wright waited near the horses, watching the men who were starting the fire. He was now convinced that, guilty or not guilty, the homesteaders would be blamed for this.

Chapter Eleven

"Ashworth's Posse"

As the minutes dragged past, Wright realized what a serious case Nugent was building against Jim, Red, and Mike. This camp was used by most of the county, at least by all those that let their steers graze the flats. Building a new shelter for their crews would be a big job and an expense, since lumber would have to be hauled from town and all those outfits would have to contribute labor. The brand owners concerned weren't likely to deal easily with whoever was responsible for the fire.

Wright was mulling this over in his mind when a shot rang out from one of the men with a lantern down by the pond. He pointed out across the black stretch of water and yelled: "There's somethin' lyin' out there. Looks like a can. And there's oil on the water."

As Wright and the others hurried down toward him, this man set his lantern on the ground, pulled off his boots, and waded out into the water. He stopped twenty feet out, where the water was waist-deep, and stooped to reach for something, his head nearly going under. Then he straightened, pulling a big five-gallon can above the surface. He held it up, water spouting from several holes in it.

"Punched holes in it so it'd sink," someone near Wright said solemnly. "The next good rain would've washed enough silt into the bottom to cover it up."

"Anyone know who this belongs to?" Nugent asked.

Folger, the Emporium clerk, spoke up. "It's new. I sold one like it to this stranger, Lance, a couple weeks ago." As all eyes swung around on him, he frowned, obviously trying to remember something. Then, abruptly: "Bring it over. I think I can tell if it's the one Lance bought."

The man in the water waded to the edge of the pond and handed the can to the clerk. He turned it bottom side up and, stepping over to a lantern, examined the price mark penciled on the galvanized metal.

"This is the one I sold Lance," he said abruptly. "Here, take a look. It was marked a dollar ninety-five, twenty cents more than it should've been. I spotted the mistake when Lance bought it and crossed out that price and wrote the right one. See?"

They saw. Several of them muttered angrily. Harvey Wright, hurt and disappointed, turned away and walked up the slope toward the trees, where the horses were tied. He wanted to get away from here, to forget his mistake in judging Jim Lance. He'd been a fool ever to want to help those three get their start.

He was reaching out to pull loose the knot in his reins when a soft, drawling voice said close by: "Looks like we'll be gettin' our necks stretched, don't it, Wright?"

The rancher stiffened, looking quickly behind him. The others were well out of hearing, still standing by the pond. He turned, peered hard into the shadows, and saw Jim Lance's tall shape standing against the thick stem of a cottonwood.

"Better make tracks," Wright said curtly. "They'll be headed for your place in about five minutes!"

"Who said we were runnin'?" came Jim's soft query.

"Damn it! You pulled a boner doin' this, Lance. Maybe you had a right wantin' to get even, but you sure picked the wrong way."

"You think we did it, then?"

"Didn't you?"

"No. We were supposed to meet Nugent's men here this afternoon. They didn't show up. Right after we ate, I got to thinkin' Nugent had tolled us across here to get us out of the way so he could wreck our place. So I talked Red and Mike into headin' back. That's where Nugent outguessed me. He must've known we'd do exactly what we did. We were almost home when we saw the fire. I sent Mike on, and Red and I came back. Red's waitin' out a ways."

Wright looked toward the group down by the pond again. It was beginning to break up. Several men were headed this way, toward their horses.

"I can't argue against this pack," the rancher said quickly. "They're sore. What'll I do?"

"You've got to keep these town men away from our place tonight," Jim told him. "Nugent wants an excuse to run us out. He'll probably fire the cabin. If he does, we begin settin' fire to some powder. It'd be a shame if the wrong men got in the way."

"But, listen, man . . . nobody could talk them out of it now."

"You'll have to figure a way. Red and I will keep you in sight, if we can, and see what luck you have. If this whole mob heads for our layout, we'll get there first. And we'll fight anyone that lifts a hand against us."

Wright saw Jim's vague shape melt into

the heavy shadow of the trees' wide trunks. A moment later he heard the slur of the Texan's boots going away. Then a man came up behind him, growling: "Harvey, we're goin' back for guns. Damned if I'll sit by and watch a thing like this happen, even if I do think Nugent's outgrown his hat size."

"Looks bad, don't it?" Wright said noncommittally as he unknotted his reins.

"Looks to me like Nugent's been right about them homesteaders all along."

Others were approaching now. They made short work of getting ready to ride. Wright stood by watching helplessly, groping for an idea and failing to get one. When they had left the trees, he was nearly the last to go.

It wasn't until the lights of Rimrock lay barely a mile ahead that he thought of anything. Even then, he touched spur to his horse and caught up with the last riders in line with little hope of being able to do anything.

"Fred," he said to the nearest man, "I'd think twice before I went into this."

The man turned and eyed him sharply, studying his face in the faint starlight. "We got the proof, didn't we?" he growled.

"Sure. But this is a job for the law, not for a mob. When Nugent cut up that fence, we didn't send a mob after him, did we?"

Two men up ahead had tightened rein and slowed their horses to let Wright come up to them, listening to what was said.

"No," the man Wright had spoken to agreed hesitantly. "But that was different. This stranger eases in here, buys into a neat set-up, and starts crackin' the whip. I say he don't get away with it."

"What about Red? And Mike Roberts?" the old rancher insisted. "You're a good friend of them both, Fred."

"It ain't them we're after. It's Lance."

"All right, we're after Lance. But I say we ought to let Ashworth deputize a couple men and go out there and make some arrests. If the whole bunch of us storms in there, someone's liable to get hurt."

As he talked, Wright had slowed his horse's pace to a deliberate walk. And now others up ahead were falling back to hear the argument. Of the fourteen riders, eight were grouped around the speakers or within hearing as they halted in the trough of a dip the road made crossing a wide wash.

Ed Nugent was one of these. He cut in with an irritable: "You've been sidin' with those homesteaders ever since this began, Harvey. Better admit you were wrong."

"I do admit it. But I'm also using my head. I still think Ashworth ought to go out there with a couple men, ride straight in without sneakin', and make his arrests. We've got the courts to decide a thing like this. Bring those three into court and, if they're guilty, send 'em to prison."

They were all stopped now. Sheriff Ashworth, sobered by the ride, blustered: "By Tophet, I'll go out there alone and bring in all three if you pikers say so!"

"Better shut your trap before you fall into it," Wright drawled dryly. "None of us are pikers. We're sensible, law-abiding men. Sheriff, pick yourself two deputies and take 'em with you. If you run into trouble, then's the time to get up a posse."

Ashworth began to swear, but was cut off by Nugent's: "He's right, Sheriff. Pick your deputies."

The darkness hid Wright's smile as he saw Nugent take the bait. He even helped the Bar Cross owner by saying: "By rights, Ed and Starr ought to go with you. Ed's the one that's taken the lickin' tonight. He ought to be there to look after his interests."

"You don't talk me out of this, Wright!" one of the men protested. "I'm goin' with the sheriff and. . . ."

"You'll do exactly as the sheriff says," Ed Nugent interrupted. "How about it, Sheriff? Do the three of us go down there backed by the law or do you want this whole pack to ride in there and get shot up?"

Ashworth was at least sober enough to see what Nugent wanted. "Any man besides me and Nugent and Starr that goes up there before I tell him to will get a chance to think it over in jail." He glared at the riders around him. Then, pompously, he added: "Come along, you two. We'll get this done!"

As Ashworth, Nugent, and Starr left the road and started up the wash, heading toward the hills, Harvey Wright took a bandanna from his hip pocket and wiped the perspiration from his face. The past three minutes had made him tense as a wagon tongue. He'd done his part. Now it was up to Jim Lance to do his.

Red was getting anxious. As the delay grew longer, he stared uneasily down along the faint gray ribbons of the road's twin ruts toward the point where they dipped out of sight in the obscurity of the wash. The Rimrock men were down there and out of sight, had been for almost five minutes. Occasionally the sound of their raised voices would drift out across the night, unintelligible, mysterious.

Finally Red said in a hushed explosion: "Why're we taggin' along with these jaspers?

What do we care what they do? We ought to be gettin' on up to help Mike."

Jim, close by, had been looking off toward the lights of Rimrock, listening, hoping to pick up a word or two of the angry discussion going on below. Now his answer eased a little of Red's uneasiness. "I want to know how many of them are comin' after us before we head home," he said.

As he was speaking, Ed Nugent, the sheriff, and Ben Starr were leaving the townsmen and going up the wash, the hooffalls of their ponies muffled by the sandy bottom of the depression. Immediately afterward, the eleven remaining riders strung up out of the wash beyond the dip of the road, making a racket that effectively hid the sound of Nugent's going when he cut up out of the wash onto harder ground. Jim and Red followed the main body of riders on in toward town, not suspecting that Harvey Wright had already accomplished what they had been hoping he would.

It was all of forty minutes before Jim, prowling the town after the Rimrock men had racked their horses in front of the Hillside, came running back to where Red waited in the alley behind the saddle shop and vaulted into the saddle. "Nugent and Starr and the sheriff aren't down there. They must've left the others when the whole bunch stopped on the way in."

The clipped remark filled Red with instant foreboding, but in Jim's harsh tone Red Curtis read a self-condemnation and a bitterness he didn't like. So he said quickly: "Who cares? We'll still make 'em dance to our tune."

"If we do, we've got to make some fast tracks!"

Jim touched his spurs to the chestnut and led the way out the alley at a reckless, hard run. He was wishing he could be as sure of their luck as his red-headed partner.

Chapter Twelve

"Barb-Wire Boomerang"

It was near midnight when Ed Nugent pulled his horse to a stop a half mile below the line of the homesteaders' south fence and let the others come up on him. Even though this had turned out far better than he'd ever hoped — with him were Ben Starr, Ashworth, and his four 'punchers who had stayed out of sight in the bunkhouse throughout the day — he couldn't put down the feeling that he'd overlooked something, that something was going wrong. As the others were closing in around him, he thought back swiftly over each point of his plan.

Starr hadn't been seen this morning taking the coal-oil can from the barn behind the homestead cabin. His main crew was camped twenty miles south, making a genuine drag for strayed Bar Cross steers below the county line. Every man who had ridden out to 'Dobe Springs tonight, with the possible exception of Harvey Wright, was convinced the homesteaders were guilty.

Best of all, here was Ashworth with full authority under the law to arrest Lance, Curtis, and Roberts and to shoot them down if they resisted that arrest. This last possibility erased some of Nugent's uneasiness.

"Sheriff," he said now, "you and Ben and I will ride straight in to the cabin. The rest of you drift along behind and stop where the lane swings into the yard. If there's trouble, use your guns. And shoot straight."

"I don't like this, Ed!" Ashworth said worriedly. "What if . . . ?"

"Hank, you ought to sober up for a day and get your guts back!" Nugent cut in scornfully. "Now come along and let's get this done!"

He led the way in, Starr and the sheriff following closely, the others hanging back. When he was out of hearing of his men, Nugent let Ashworth come alongside.

"Hank, where are your brains?" he said hotly. "Aren't you forgettin' a few things?"

Ashworth, thus reminded of a certain understanding that lay between them, one that dated back to before election, said contritely: "Guess my think tank wasn't workin', Ed. What do I do?"

Starr was listening, too, as Nugent answered. "You're to try to toll those three out of the cabin. Make 'em show a light if you can. When they're all three in the open, Ben and I will do the rest."

"Ed, that's. . . ." Ashworth's voice failed him when he got that far.

"Murder?" Nugent taunted. "Who's goin' to know what happened? Who besides you and Ben and . . . ?"

The quick drum of hoofs far down along the trail cut in on Nugent's words. He yanked his horse to a stop and stood in stirrups to look on down the starlit meadow. He could see his own four men. But, beyond them, the darkness closed down, and he could make out no detail.

Abruptly he snapped: "This must be them! Off the trail! Ben, let 'em have it when they go past!" He swore feelingly, remembering that he was too far from his men to give them orders. "Hank, you stay out of. . . ."

Crack! Crack! Crack!

The sudden sound of guns from below drowned out Nugent's voice. Down there, he saw the tight knot of his riders all at once spread open. One lined out to the left of the trail, one stayed where he was, two more ran their horses to the right.

A six-gun's throaty roar split open the night, and the man who had gone left spilled from the saddle with a strangled cry. And now, far down to Nugent's right across the meadow, he saw two vague, hurrying shapes of riders almost even with him.

"Ben, after 'em!" he bawled. "Down there to your left!" He raked his own horse's flanks with spurs. As the animal lunged from the trail, he reached for the rifle in his saddle boot and found that the bulk of the holster high on the left side of his chest made his move awkward. He came close to taking out the gun and throwing it away or ramming it in his belt, but at the last moment he changed his mind. Then he forgot the gun as he saw Starr, slightly ahead, level his Winchester and line a shot down across the meadow.

Starr's bullet, thrown from his fast-running horse, was wildly aimed. But the luck that had failed Jim and Red a few moments ago in letting them be surprised by the four Bar Cross crewmen down the trail now failed them again. For Red's horse went down the instant after Starr's rifle exploded, pitching his rider clear and almost under the hoofs of Jim's racing chestnut.

Jim slid the chestnut to a stop, wheeled around, and rode in abreast of Red as the redhead was coming groggily to his feet. Jim reached down, threw an arm across his partner's chest, and swung Red from the ground, using spurs to drive the animal into a run again. For several seconds Jim fought against being dragged from the saddle by Red's weight. Then, with a twisting lift, the redhead managed to pull himself to the horse's back. A moment later, astride the chestnut behind Jim, he was emptying his six-gun at the two shapes rushing down at them from the trail.

As Red's gun blasted out, a quick backward glance showed Jim two things. First, the two Bar Cross men had closed to within easy range as he went back to get Red, but second, more importantly, those quick shots of Red's had made the two riders swerve apart and slowed their headlong pace.

Jim saw that now they might be able to cross the lower end of the meadow and make the trees beyond to lose their pursuers. But the chestnut was tiring fast under its double burden. Nugent and Starr would be coming at them again in a moment.

Just then Jim remembered Mike, alone at the cabin. Even though he and Red gained the safety of the timber and made good their escape, Mike would be caught — one man fighting the six or seven riders Jim had seen. It took no imagination to guess what the outcome would be. Jim had asked Mike not to leave the cabin, and his lanky, slow-speaking partner would stick there until told to do otherwise.

Jim looked toward the trail and saw the risk involved in reaching it and riding up the lane. But going that way offered one advantage. Instead of the long, killing chase across to the timber, this second chance would be decided within seconds. Recklessly, knowing he couldn't ignore Mike's danger, he took this more dangerous choice.

He reined the horse hard to the right, using left spur, and half turned in the saddle to send three swift shots at the nearest Bar Cross man as he cut directly in front of him. This was Nugent, who felt the air-whip of a bullet, bent low on the off side of his horse, and tightened rein, unnerved at Jim's unexpected rush up the slope toward him.

All at once Nugent's horse broke stride as a second bullet burned the animal's neck. Suddenly Nugent was afraid. Now, instead of closing in on the two homesteaders for a sure shot, he swerved even farther from their path. Behind, coming up fast, Ben Starr bawled stridently — "Don't let 'em get away, Ed!" — and cut loose with his .30-30.

But Ed Nugent had felt the closeness of death and didn't want to feel it a second time. Momentarily unnerved, he swerved and held his distance while the chestnut pounded past less than five rods away, making for the trail and the head of the lane, close above.

Jim breathed a sigh of relief as he saw Nugent slow and turn aside. Swinging around in the saddle, he lined his gun over Red's shoulder and shot once at Starr, coming up beyond Nugent. Then he reined the chestnut into the trail. He had a chance now, a better chance than the timber across the meadow would have offered.

The gate posts came up out of the blurred obscurity ahead. Jim saw the mound of tangled wire as a shapeless shadow close to the left gate post. Somehow, sight of that worthless wire tightened Jim's hatred for Nugent as even the bullets of the last minute had failed to do. Close behind he could hear the drum of hoofs as not only Starr and Nugent gained on him but were joined by three other riders who had been left down the meadow. And here ahead was the symbol of Nugent's victory, that tangled mass of wire.

It looked as though Nugent would win, after all. In his concentration on outwitting Nugent and Starr, Jim had forgotten the Bar Cross crewmen, who had run straight up the trail. This reckless chance he had taken to reach the cabin and fort up there had been a foolish move.

A rifle exploded over the chestnut's hoof pound, and Jim heard Red groan. He turned and looked at his partner. Red's face was tight with pain, and he held his left shoulder with his gun hand. But he only smiled crookedly and said: "Give me a minute and I'll be all right."

Jim knew Red was lying. His partner was badly hurt. Looking beyond Red, he saw another gun back there stab flame against the darkness. Two riders were close enough so that he could see them plainly.

His glance whipped ahead again. The gate was close now, the mound of barbed wire no longer shapeless but clear in outline.

Suddenly Jim thought of something. Ramming his Colt into holster, he reached down to pull loose the knot of the thong that held his rope to the swell of the saddle. Quickly he pulled the coiled rope free and shook out the loop in it.

There was barely time to swing the rope's small loop in a single tight circle over his head before making the cast. He saw the loop snake out toward the mound of barbed wire and then trail out of sight in the faint light as he came abreast of the wire. An instant later he felt the rope catch and hold. Then, slowing the horse, he ran out the slack in the rope and felt it tighten suddenly across his thigh. He threw two quick turns around the horn, brought home his spurs, and ran his horse in through the gate.

The chestnut slowed abruptly under the added weight it was pulling. Looking back,

Jim saw the mound of wire slowly changing shape. There were now tangled coils of wire trailing out from the end of his rope and in through the gate. Back there two guns cracked out. A searing pain cut across Jim's left upper arm as the riders rushed up out of the obscurity, closing on the gate fast.

As the leading rider back there raced to be first through the gate, Jim let go the rope and saw it whip away and down. The chestnut seemed to leap ahead, and Jim let him run half a dozen more strides before pulling him in to a quick stop. Then, deliberately, he shucked shells from his belt and began reloading the Colt.

Suddenly from behind came a horse's high-pitched neighing followed by a man's shrill yell of pain. Only when Red breathed a solemn, awed oath did Jim look back.

That first rider was down, howling in pain as he writhed in the tangle of wire choking the mouth of the lane. His horse was still on his feet, thrashing and trying to lunge out of the entangling wire. Beyond, two riders cut into the head of the lane abreast and at a hard run. The horse on the left suddenly had his forefeet swept from under him by the wire, throwing his rider against the fence. The other, feeling the wire strike his forelegs, all at once began pitching. The second rider fell sideways from the saddle and was trampled as Nugent, close behind, pressed on.

Jim sat grimly silent, hating what he'd done but knowing it had saved them. Red said: "Jumpin' Jupiter, what a sight!" A moment later, Jim lined his gun and shot down an injured horse as two more riders, Ashworth one of them, ran their horses into the jam. It was so dark that those last two hadn't been able to make out the cause of the confusion ahead.

Red was looking at Jim, and what he saw on his partner's face made him say quickly: "You had to do it, man! I know you hate it. But it was them or us. Let's beat it."

Jim said only: "We'd better stick around and see if we can help."

But there was nothing they could do to help. Only the last Bar Cross rider was able to see in time what was ahead and swing aside to avoid the trap.

When Jim saw that one of the downed men was on his feet and unhurt, he said: "Let's go get Mike and ride. They won't come any farther right now."

"Where we headed?"

"Town," was Jim's answer. "Nugent will go there to gather up a posse when he gets himself untangled. We'll be there when he does. And maybe we can get this settled before he gets that mob organized and headed out here to finish us off." He turned and glanced at Red's shoulder. "How's the arm?"

"Not so bad now," Red said honestly. "I'll wrap it up and be good for the rest of the night."

"Sure you're all right?"

Red grinned. "After that lickin' we gave Nugent? Feller, I couldn't be better."

Chapter Thirteen

"Trial by Lead"

Ordinarily only a light or two marked the town of Rimrock at two in the morning. This morning, however, the settlement looked like a fallen cluster of brightly winking stars at that early hour. Every house but the few empty ones had lamps burning, and several of the stores were as brightly lighted as on a dark and rainy Saturday afternoon.

At the hardware store men formed a line from the front door all the way to the back counter, waiting to buy shells. At the livery barn the ramp was cluttered with restive horses either being saddled or standing tied, waiting for their riders. The hostler couldn't seem to make any order from the confusion and kept bawling: "Get those jugheads out onto the street and give us room to work in here!"

The Hillside, open for business and selling more whisky than it had on last election night, was crowded to the doors. The jam was thickest around the pool table. There, lying on a tarp hastily thrown across the table to save the green felt from stain, were three men. Ben Starr was one, Henry Ashworth another, and a Bar Cross crewman the third. The left side of Starr's face was gashed from ear to chin and his shoulder on that side was torn badly. His crewman's right pant leg was ripped from mid-thigh to ankle, exposing a criss-crossing of deep gashes. But Henry Ashworth was worse off. He had broken his right arm in his fall, and two deep cuts along the thick muscle of his back made him groan every time he moved. Just now Doc Morehouse had given him a stiff shot of whisky and was ready to take stitches in his back.

Harvey Wright stood across the table from Ed Nugent, whose left arm was in a sling and whose red, welted face showed traces of his encounter with the barbed wire. In the past minutes Wright had been trying to knock holes in Nugent's story of what had happened, even though the rest of the town was working itself up to a lynching.

"You say Lance and his partners lined you up at the point of guns, then shot at your horses and ran them into this line of wire, Nugent?" he asked.

Ashworth, needing courage for his coming ordeal, blustered: "Go take a look at my horse if you don't believe it, Harvey! It was the damnedest, most cold-blooded thing I ever run against! Them three are devils, I tell you!"

"What was Newell doing there?" Wright asked, referring to the hurt Bar Cross crewman lying on the table near the sheriff.

Nugent's stare at the older man was stony. "I told you once that Newell and the three others came back while I was gone. That job the crew is doin' down south is taking longer than I'd counted on. They came back for more grub."

"But why four of them?" Wright asked patiently. "It takes only one man to load a buckboard and drive it."

An angry mutter of disapproval came from the close-packed listeners. Wright paid that no attention. He didn't know what good he was doing trying to make Nugent out a liar, but he knew Nugent was lying and had been all night.

Nugent shrugged and looked at the others. "Hell, do I have to stand here defendin' myself like a kid caught stealin' apples?"

An angry murmur of assent sounded out across the room, and one man, standing close to Wright, said sourly: "Better watch your step, Wright, or we'll be thinkin' you had something to do with this."

Harvey Wright knew the spot he was in but ignored it. "You're sure it was Jim Lance that

119

bragged on how they'd fired your camp?" he asked.

"He was as cool as a bucket of ice," Ben Starr put in, as he pushed up onto one elbow. "He wouldn't have done it, of course, if he expected we was going to get away alive."

"Just how did you manage to get away?" Wright queried. "I don't think you mentioned that."

Starr looked at Nugent who said merely: "We can take that up later, after we've strung up those three."

"Why not take it up now, Nugent?" asked a voice from the direction of the wall beyond the pool table.

Wright swung around, as did the others. There, beside the open window he'd just stepped through, stood Jim Lance. He had a horn-handled .38 in his hand. The gun was aimed toward the floor, carelessly.

At the back of the crowd in the direction of the bar, men began to shift furtively. All at once there came the crash of falling glass from the front window. Through the broken-out lower sash stepped Red Curtis, left arm in a sling and a gun in his good hand.

"Stay set, gents," he said warningly, "and no one's goin' to be diggin' any graves in the mornin'!"

Immediately the back fringe of the crowd

stopped its motion.

"Just in case," Jim drawled. "Mike Roberts is right by the alley door with a shotgun."

His glance went to the pool table and beyond it. "Now, Nugent, we're listenin'. How did you get away from our place without my cuttin' your heart out and pullin' off your legs and arms?"

A tense, expectant silence settled over the room. Men whose anger had been fanned to a white heat against the homesteaders looked to Nugent for an answer. And in his hesitation they saw quickly that the things he had been telling them these past twenty minutes weren't all true.

"We're waitin'," Jim drawled, as Nugent made no answer.

Finally Nugent swung part way around and faced the thickest gathering of the crowd. "Are we going to let him get away with this?" he called loudly. "Why doesn't someone make a try for him?"

"Give him an answer, Nugent," Harvey Wright said.

Perhaps the words of the old rancher did more than anything else to convince the listeners that Nugent had been lying about the details of what had happened at the homestead. Until now, Wright had only made a nuisance of himself, by doubting Nugent's word. But abruptly men were remembering that Harvey Wright was a shrewd, honest man and that they should have listened to him in the first place.

Slowly the mob was having a change of mind. A moment ago few men in the room would have hesitated in shooting Jim down if they had the chance. Now they almost ignored him and shifted their attention to Nugent.

"Maybe you need some remindin', Nugent," Jim drawled. "For instance, that coal-oil can you fished out of the pond at the springs. It was stolen from our barn today after we left. Starr, how about it? You ought to remember."

Ben Starr was sitting up now, legs over the edge of the table. "This ain't gettin' you nothin', Lance," he said in a surly tone.

Jim lazily rocked his gun into line. "Remember that first day, Starr?" he asked tonelessly. His glance lifted a trifle. "Now I'd say your hair's gettin' a little thick there at the sides." He looked beyond the Bar Cross man. "You gents there behind Starr better move away before I begin my barberin' job on him."

Beyond the table men moved hastily out of line. Starr heard that, and sweat gathered on his forehead. His eyes were riveted to Jim's Colt, fascinated by the round bore of the barrel and the lean hand that held it lined.

Jim saw what Starr was watching and, slowly, put his thumb to the hammer and drew it back. "Which side do you part your hair on?" he said casually. "I forget, Starr."

The hammer clicked, and Jim's thumb moved off it.

"Don't let him bluff you, Ben!" Ed Nugent said suddenly. His words steeled the Bar Cross foreman, whose lips curled down to shape a sneer.

"Go ahead, Lance," Nugent drawled, smiling.

Hardly had his words died when Jim's gun exploded in a concussion that made the lamp over the table flicker. Starr gave a hoarse bellow and lifted his right hand to the side of his head where, a moment ago, he had felt a light touch against his scalp. His hand came away holding several shreds of his dark hair. He looked at them, and his face went deathly pale.

"Don't, Ben!" Nugent snapped, as he saw his foreman's nerve begin to crumble. Then, to Jim: "What's this gettin' you, Lance? You can make a man confess to anything if you threaten his life." He looked around at the crowd. "Sure, Ben'll say he swiped that coal-oil can from Lance's barn. How many of you wouldn't, with the threat of gettin' a slug

123

through his guts if he didn't?"

Jim sensed the crowd turning undecided again. They had been ignoring him. Now he felt their attention coming back to him questioning, wanting conviction.

He was trying to think of another way of forcing Starr's confession when the crowd over by the swing doors stirred and a restless murmur of talk sprang up there. In a moment Jim heard Ralph Pope's ordinarily mild voice raised in sharp command. A moment later, Ralph, his thinning hair wind-blown, his breathing deep and quick, roughly elbowed his way through the crowd to the cleared space around the pool table.

His quick glance took in Jim, the gun in Jim's hand, and Starr and Nugent. His ordinarily mild manner was missing as he asked Jim: "Have they owned up to it yet?"

"Starr's memory's gone back on him," Jim drawled. "We're tryin' to get him to remember that he swiped something from us this morning."

Pope's stare swung around hard on the Bar Cross foreman. His eyes glinted with anger and puzzlement. Then, abruptly, he was saying: "I don't know what this is leadin' to, but you might as well admit you were on our place this morning, Starr. I know because I saw you headed up through the trees with what looked like a bucket or a milk can tied on behind your saddle." Pope's glance went to Jim again. "Does that help any, Jim?"

"It's a frame-up!" snarled Ben Starr. "Lance primed Pope to come in here and run this sandy on me!"

"Ralph," Jim drawled, "tell them when you last saw me."

"Not for about a week, I reckon," Pope said, frowning as he tried to remember. "It must've been the day of the meetin' here in town. Last night I got to thinkin' I wasn't doin' my share out there at the place. So I asked for the day off and rode out thinkin' you could put me to work. I cut in through timber and was ridin' down on the meadow across from the cabin when I saw Starr headed up into the trees opposite. I didn't think much of it till I found no one was at the cabin. I been worried about it all day."

"What about tonight, Ralph?" Jim asked. "Has anyone told you what happened?"

Pope shook his head. "Nope. Right after supper I went out to the place again. The cabin was still empty. I was comin' back when I saw a fire out in the direction of 'Dobe Springs on the flats. Feelin' like I did, sort o' fiddle-footed and worryin' about you boys, I thought I'd swing out there and see what was wrong. By the time I rode down on the

125

springs, the fire had pretty near burned out. I was goin' to take a look when I sees a jasper goin' off like he didn't want to be seen. Pretty soon he got between me and what light there was left, and I seen it was Starr." The look Pope gave Jim was puzzled. "You better tell me what's wrong, Jim. I'd be glad to help you with anything I can."

Jim's face took on a thin smile. "You've helped just about enough, Ralph," he drawled. He looked at Nugent. "Wouldn't you say so, Nugent?"

A change had come over the Bar Cross owner's face. It relaxed out of the tightness it had hardened into as Ralph Pope spoke. He lifted his hands. "You win," he said resignedly.

"Someone get his iron," Jim ordered.

A man stepped in behind Nugent and lifted the .45 from his holster. Grimacing, Sheriff Ashworth got down from the table and took out a pair of handcuffs from his pocket.

Someone said — "Better use 'em on yourself, Hank." — and the tension that had been holding the crowd suddenly broke. The onlookers broke into a riotous guffawing. Jim, seeing several men closing in on Nugent, holstered his gun as Wright stepped over to him and warmly gripped his hand.

As Jim's glance swung away, Nugent suddenly shouldered hard the men closest to him and lunged in toward a cleared space by the table. As he moved, his hand stabbed in under his arm sling and his canvas coat.

Out of the corner of his eye, Jim saw Nugent's lunge. He snatched his hand from Wright's tight grasp, spun around, and stabbed hand to holster. The man Nugent had knocked aside bawled — "Look out!" — and the crowd froze.

From the front of the room Red Curtis saw the swift drop of Jim's hand as Nugent was pulling his gun clear. He saw Jim's holster tilt up, saw flame stab from it at the instant Nugent's gun arced down and exploded. Then Jim's gun swung clear of leather, and he shot again. Red's glance whipped to Nugent.

The big man was doubled over, yet trying to line the short-barreled gun he had pulled from his shoulder holster. Sheer agony was etched on his face that had gone suddenly pale. Blood flecked on his lips. His gun all at once exploded downward, the bullet chipping off a corner of the table leg.

Ed Nugent staggered forward, the table caught him, and he fell out across it. Then, his big body going slack, the weight of his buckling legs dragged him off the table, and he hit the floor hard, rolling onto his back.

An awed silence held the room. And now

the air was strong with the acrid smell of cordite.

It was Harvey Wright who ended the silence. "That ought to settle it," he said, and his words prophesied a new era in which cowman and homesteader could live in peace and prosperity. "When a man is as greedy for land as Ed Nugent was, he pays a dear price for it."

His eyes reflecting the regret he felt, Jim holstered his weapon. Others in the room were now staring at Nugent's foreman, his anger and puzzlement having turned to fear.

"I jest worked for him and did what I was told," Ben Starr muttered lamely.

"Maybe so," Wright said, "but right now I suggest we get Ed up off the floor and prepare him for a proper burial."

Several men leaped forward to help. Jim moved over to the bar where he was joined by Red Curtis, Mike Roberts, and Ralph Pope. They drank in silence, as if each of them realized that a dear price had also been paid for peace.

CLAIMING OF THE DEERFOOT

CHAPTER ONE

Through the driving downpour of the rain, Ed Thorn surveyed Ledge's uptilted muddy street, the sodden huddle of tar paper and log shacks, and had the feeling that this boom camp represented his last chance at honest living. For eight months now bad luck had dogged him as insistently as his daylight shadow, as certainly as each sleep's nightmare. Nothing but a stubborn pride had brought him up here to make one final attempt at living with a name that been ruined that day in Montana when, along an obscure trail, he had lost stage, shotgun guard, and bullion shipment. It was that pride that made him cling to his name, refuse to take another. His one hope now was that in this strange country his name would mean nothing.

Numbed by the cold and wet to the skin even though he wore a poncho, utterly weary under the load of a double-rigged saddle he'd lugged these last four miles since dark, a small and warm excitement ran through him as he

131

squinted into the darkness trying to read the names lettered on the store fronts immediately ahead. The faint sound of laughter blended with the tinny off-key beat of a piano rising above the steady drone of the rain told him that the squat tar paper shack with the four lighted windows to his left was the saloon, that life went on here even though the walks flanking the street's muddy trough were as deserted as a ghost town's. He made out an assayer's sign beyond the saloon, a harness maker's, and a hotel's this side of it. His glance swung sharply right and there, plainly lettered across a broad window of a log building, was the legend he sought: **Deerfoot Stage Line**.

He lifted his sucking boots and plodded head down against the slashing fog of rain to the plank walk in front of the stage station. There he spent a deliberate half minute cleaning the mud from his boots and spurs. Finished, he heaved the saddle more squarely onto his back and turned toward the door. Through the window he had a momentary glimpse of the room inside, relishing the promised warmth of its big hogback stove.

He saw something else, too. Three people were in the room, two men and a girl. One man, big-framed and grizzled, sat in a swivel chair before a roll-top desk, head down and apparently studying his hands that rested folded on the desk top. In the fleeting instant Ed Thorn looked in there, this man spoke without raising his glance. The girl, standing while leaning against the desk toward the room's front, made a reply, the expression on her face coldly sober. The room's third occupant, a lanky, narrow-faced man of middle age sitting on a cot in the room's far corner, back to wall, lifted his left arm in a gesture expressing plain helplessness. His right arm hung limply in a sling.

Ed Thorn paused a moment before stepping to the door. It hadn't been his intention to eavesdrop, but that one glance into the room, seeing the mute interchange of word and expression on the faces within, brought out all too clearly the fact that those three were held by a common intensity of feeling, one that was strangely bleak and real. For a moment only he considered this. Then he forgot it in the desire to make the most of his chance.

Stepping in through the full-height door, he had to duck his head to save his wide-brimmed Stetson a crushing on the frame. The rush of wind that came with him made the lamp's flame on the desk's high shelf flicker uncertainly. He swung his saddle to the floor and backed into the door, pushing it shut, drawling:

"Down below they told me there was a job here . . . for a driver. I was to ask to see Tom Hunter."

"I'm Hunter," said the oldster at the desk. His square and sun-blackened face remained impassive as he studied Ed. There was no sign of welcome in his expression. At length his voice intoned levelly: "You're about three hours too late."

Ed was unbuckling his poncho. His glance left Hunter and went to the girl. He realized abruptly that even with her utterly grave expression she was beautiful with the lamplight edging her tawny blonde head with spun pale gold. He looked toward the man on the cot, and saw that he was being regarded with an expression barely removed from hostility.

He said: "I couldn't help that. My jughead broke a leg when the trail caved under him." When he saw that his explanation had little effect, a small irritation rose up in him and he bridled. "No one said anything about killin' myself getting here."

The girl was the first to break from her reserve. She smiled at him, as though in apology. "You'll have to forgive us," she said. "What Dad means is that three hours ago, a driver would have had a chance to get a stage through. Now there isn't a chance, with the washes running and the trail gone."

"Then why didn't a driver leave three hours ago?" Ed Thorn asked.

Her smile held as she nodded to the man on the cot: "Dan, here, stopped a bullet his last trip down. He can't drive with one arm. Dad doesn't drive, and our other man has been sick two days with a cold threatening to turn into pneumonia. So it looks like we lost our contract."

"Contract?"

Tom Hunter's deep voice boomed: "Mail. We're running a trial schedule for three months, with only ten days to go before getting a five-year contract. I was fool enough to think I could swing it."

"Why can't you?" Ed queried.

"Because of twenty words," Hunter answered in thinly veiled sarcasm. "A damned twenty word clause that gives me only a ten-hour leeway from my schedule due to weather, washed-out trails, or breakage in equipment." He shrugged his massive shoulders in a helpless gesture and let out a weary sigh. "Well, I can always go into the freightin' business."

For long seconds an eloquent silence ran through the room, intensified by the monotonous and muted drone of the rain on the roof. Ed was aware of two things: that the losing of the mail contract would be a severe blow to

135

Tom Hunter and that here was the chance he himself had been waiting for. His thoughts went back to his ride this afternoon, picturing the vicissitudes of the trail that long habit made him remember clearly. At length, he said: "How much time have you?"

Hunter's glance came up to meet him. "Until two in the mornin', counting the extra ten hours."

"Then get the teams hitched. I'll take a stage through." Ed paused a moment, then asked: "Any passengers to go down?"

Behind him, the man on the cot said solemnly: "A hundred dollars couldn't hire one passenger to take that trip tonight. They'd. . . ."

"Then get me a buckboard and your best team."

Once again the weighty silence held them. In the brief interval, a light of hope came to the girl's eyes, a questioning one to her father's. Then the man on the cot said: "There's only two men I've ever heard of could drive that forty miles in a storm like this even if they knew the trail. One's Ben O'Daniels, and he's been dead twenty years. The other's Ed Thorn, damn his rotten soul!"

Quick anger settled through Ed and was gone an instant later. He wheeled slowly to face the driver, drawling: "I'll forget you said

136

that last. I'm Ed Thorn."

Behind him at the desk, the swivel chair grated against the floor planks. He had a brief warning in the girl's sharp cry — "Dad!" — and turned to face the desk in time to see Tom Hunter's massive bulk come charging up out of the chair. The stage owner's blunt face was set in a grimace of rage, and his two fists were knotted, arms half raised. He took two swift steps that put him almost within reach of Ed. Then, standing spraddle-legged, his harsh voice grated: "You're Thorn, and you dare show your face here? My God, you stepped into it without knowin'! Think, Thorn! Remember that kid ridin' guard up in Montana, the one you lost with the bullion? He was mine. Bob Hunter!"

A fast-settling paralysis of surprise and sheer helplessness took its hold on Ed Thorn. In that moment Tom Hunter ignored his daughter's frightened cry and swung his right fist, stepping in. Ed saw the blow coming and rolled with it a fraction of a second too late. It ripped along his jaw and into his neck, lifting him back off his feet in a turning sprawl. He hit the boards on his left shoulder, too dazed to brace himself to the impact. His head snapped back and hit the floor with a sickeningly hard thud. For an instant he fought frantically to retain his fading senses and failed as pain and a white blaze of light blotted out his consciousness.

Thorn woke to the chill bite of cold water running down his face. When he opened his eyes, he found his body sitting, sagged in a chair. A rough hand took a grip on his hair and jerked his head up. He was looking into Tom Hunter's anger-hardened face. Beyond Hunter stood the girl, and to one side of her Ed could see Hunter's driver, a smile of satisfaction imprinted on his narrow face.

Suddenly, without warning, Tom Hunter struck him an open-handed blow in the face. It jarred Ed almost to insensibility and would have knocked him to the floor but for the stage owner's hold on his hair. As the sharp pain of the blow drove in on Ed, a riot of anger took him. He opened his eyes to see Hunter's hand swinging in at him again. With a convulsive jerk, he wrenched his head free and rolled out of the chair. Two strides put him out of Hunter's reach. He ripped open the poncho and whipped it off as Hunter charged in at him. Swinging the poncho around, he threw it fully in Hunter's face.

Hunter stopped abruptly, clawing the wet mass of oil-skinned cloth from his face. When he had thrown it aside and raised his hands once again, Ed cocked his long body and

138

lunged. His right fist drove solidly into Hunter's middle. The stage owner grunted in pain and doubled up. Ed's uppercut caught him that way, on the point of the jaw, rocking him back on his heels. Then, too swiftly timed for the eye to follow, Ed struck twice. His right, starting low, traveled through a long arc and crushed solidly at Hunter's ear, tilting the stage owner's head sideways. His left, hard on the heel of the first blow, rocked Hunter's head upright once more.

Hunter swayed uncertainly and all at once fell to his knees, braced by outstretched hands. Ed saw the man's shaggy head sag and only then stepped back, breathing hard. Then, behind him, he heard a small, furtive sound. Barely in time, he remembered Hunter's driver and wheeled to one side, facing about in time to see a chair arcing down at him, its back gripped in the driver's one good hand. One chair leg glanced off Ed's shoulder. He swung his right, hard, catching the driver off balance. His blow ripped a gash along the driver's right cheekbone, and its force lifted the man's frail weight from the floor and sent him to one side in a lurching sprawl. He skidded along the floor until finally he sat with back to wall.

The driver shook his head to clear his senses. Then, with an oath, his free hand clawed to his belt where he wore a gun thrust through the waistband of his trousers. Ed lunged in, kicking hard with a boot that hit the man on the wrist, weapon half drawn. The gun spun out of the driver's grasp and connected with the floor with a sharp thud and skidded to the room's front wall.

Ed stepped back. The girl, oval face pale and eyes wide in fear, stood with her back to the wall across the room by the desk, one clenched hand to her mouth as though stifling a cry. Tom Hunter now sat in the middle of the floor, head on knees and arms hanging limply to the floor beside him. The driver, senses steady now, pushed back away from Ed along the wall.

Ed let his glance go slowly between the three of them before he drawled: "I don't blame you, Hunter, not even for striking a man when he's out. But, damn you, you'll listen to what I have to say. I didn't sell out my owners up there in Montana. I didn't kill Bob. I was framed."

Hunter's head came up slowly off his knees. Along the right side of his jaw a livid bruise glowed redly. His eyes mirrored a hateful look as he glared at Ed and said: "Nan, there's a gun in the top drawer. Reach it and pass it to me."

"No, Dad," the girl said quickly. "Ed

140

Thorn, get out of here!"

Ed ignored her, said: "Hunter, you'll listen to this before I leave. Two days before Bob and I started out with that bullion, Bill Prall, the line's manager, brought two men to me, claimin' they were agents for the insurance outfit covering the shipment. He said they'd talk over extra pay with me, since we were carrying a hundred thousand in gold and there was some risk. Those two offered me two thousand to make the trip, paid me in advance. I banked the money. Besides that, they told me the trail to follow. I took that trail along with the three extra guards Prall furnished me. Ten miles out those guards threw down on us. They shot Bob in the back, gun-whipped me. When it was all over, it was my word against Bill Prall's. . . ."

"The hell with this!" cut in Hunter's driver, getting awkwardly to his feet. "You were in with the bunch that took the gold. Ed Thorn, the best man that ever held the ribbons, selling out!"

Ed glanced once at the driver, then ignored him, continuing: "Bill Prall claimed he'd never brought in those two insurance men, said he didn't know a thing about the guards nor about the trail we took. It was a frame-up, and he was in on it. I didn't kill Bob, didn't have a chance even to help him."

Hunter looked helplessly about the room, and his glance settled on the gun lying at the front wall. He started crawling toward it on hands and knees. Ed stepped over there, picked up the weapon, and went to the door. He opened it and tossed the gun into the street. When he'd closed the door again and faced Hunter once more, the stage owner was on his feet, swaying uncertainly.

Hunter said: "For the love of God, Nan, get me that iron out of the desk."

The girl didn't move. She was eyeing Ed now in a strange, calculating way, head held proudly erect. All at once she breathed: "Why do you bother to talk about it, Ed Thorn? What is it getting you? Why don't you leave?"

The thought that lay behind her words, her utter disbelief, was the thing that convinced Ed most strongly of his failure. In the next few seconds, under the hard glances of these three, he tasted all the bitterness of defeat. Here, facing him now, were two people who had loved the Bob Hunter he had once thought of almost as a brother. The intense hatred and loathing in their glances drove home the feeling of helplessness that had ridden with him these past eight months. Once again his pride in not hiding his name had cheated him, driven him further along a downward trail that seemed to have no ending.

Slowly, something in him rebelled. Before he had even recognized the seed of the idea that took root in his brain, he was stooping down and unlacing the pouch of his saddle. From the pouch he lifted out a pair of heavy belts and holsters sheathing twin .45s. He swung them about his waist, tying the holster thongs low at his thighs. Then, palming out one gun, he leveled it at Hunter's driver, saying harshly: "You'll come along to show me the bad spots. Right now we're getting a team hitched to the lightest rig in your barn. Get movin'!"

Hunter moved uncertainly toward the desk. Ed crossed the room in three strides, coming between the stage owner and the desk. He hefted the gun in his hand. "Don't make me rip open your head with this, Hunter!" Then, nodding toward the room's rear door, he said to the driver: "Get out there to the stables."

The driver's glance narrowed, and his jaw set stubbornly. The girl was quick to say: "Better go, Dan. If he's fool enough to want to prove something by trying to help us, let him."

Dan moved across the room then, sullenly, his left hand clenching his hurt right shoulder that had been jarred by his fall and was clearly paining him. He took a lantern from a peg on the back wall near the door, put it on a low shelf, and levered it open. As he wiped a match alight on the seat of his pants and touched it to the lantern's wick, he smiled thinly, mockingly, at Ed and said: "Sure, Thorn. If you're loco enough to think you're provin' something, we'll take all the help you want to give."

Chapter Two

For six hours, along forty miles of obscure trail, Dan Belden lived through a prolonged hell that night. It began bare seconds after they'd dropped the lights of Ledge behind them along the cañon trail, and it didn't let up until Ed Thorn was trotting Tom Hunter's team of mud-splashed and badly blown Morgans along Plainsville's wide main street shortly after one o'clock.

It was hell for many reasons. One was that Dan's injured shoulder was aching with each jolt of the buckboard and that he needed his good arm to hold onto the seat brace. Another was that after the first three minutes of going he lost the desire to take the ribbons in his own hands and began trusting the surest, quickest pair of hands he'd ever seen on the reins, wishing with a deep and awful longing that it could be he and not Ed Thorn who possessed this amazing way with horses.

Not once in those six hours had Ed Thorn

spoken a word, either to Dan Belden or to the horses. The fact that Thorn could exact precise obedience to his will by whip and pressure on the reins alone, abandoning the time-worn obscenity of all drivers, amazed Dan Belden from the beginning. He himself cursed violently when they struck heavy going, where he would have sworn that no man could have the eyes to see the trail ahead and do the right thing at precisely the right instant. A flick of the reins, a touch with the whip on the geldings' rumps, a quick shifting of the body's weight countless times meant the difference between keeping two wheels on the trail or plunging a hundred feet to the bottom of the ever-narrowing cañon, and Ed Thorn each time invariably acted with smooth perfection.

It was at Saw Tooth Wash that Dan Belden in ninety interminable seconds lived through more stark and real fear than an accumulation of all he had before experienced in his fifty years of precarious living. By the time they struck Saw Tooth, a narrow and treacherous wash coming out of a high offshoot to the main cañon, the rain had stopped and the sky had cleared enough to give them faint starlight to see by. That starlight made it all the worse, for its reflection eerily whitened the seventy-foot-wide foaming, roaring mass of water that poured from the offshoot into the main cañon.

"Can't do it!" he'd yelled, hand cupped to Thorn's ear, seeing that onrushing flood.

Then, even before he could take his hand down and reach for the seat brace, Thorn had brought the whip down across the rumps of the team and sent them breast high into the nearest upcurling wave of the torrent. Had Dan had the presence of mind to jump, he would have left the buckboard there, for Thorn was driving like a madman, taking impossible chances, or so it seemed.

Ed Thorn hadn't headed straight across Saw Tooth, giving the current a broadside chance at overturning the buckboard. Instead, he'd put the team up into the offshoot mouth, driving obliquely against the boiling mass of water. Once he'd sensed the presence of a hole and reined the team around it barely in time for the off gelding to keep its footing. Another time he'd seen the shadow of a ten-foot-high tree bole loom, rolling out of the darkness directly at them, and brought the team to a stand in time for the wheeling mass of earth and roots to roll ponderously by barely a foot beyond the team's noses. Then, deep in the gloom of Saw Tooth's mouth and with the towering walls rising sheerly from the water to cut off their last chances of escape, he'd turned the team on a narrow shallows and raced the current down and out and onto the firm trail. Looking back, after Thorn had stopped on safe ground to blow the team, Dan Belden wasn't at all sure that the crossing hadn't been an illusion, that he wouldn't wake in a few moments and find himself sweating in the clutches of a nightmare in his bunk at the rear of Tom Hunter's stage station in Ledge.

After crossing Saw Tooth, Dan had become immune to fright. A solid diet of it for the last ten miles, over places where they had to get down and lift the off wheels over the drop-offs, convinced Dan that Ed Thorn was possessed of an unbeatable streak of luck and that so long as he was near Thorn nothing could happen to him.

Now, glancing sideways at Thorn as they went along Plainsville's wide street, Dan couldn't help but voice his admiration by saying: "Nice job, Thorn. We're in time."

The only answer he got was a brief nod. A quarter minute later they were turning into the wide maw of the feed barn's door, hearing a sleepy but surprised hostler say: "God Almighty! Is it you, Dan? How the hell'd you get here? Fly?"

"Ask him," Dan said, nodding to Ed Thorn and climbing stiffly aground. As an afterthought, he added: "He's our new driver, name's Ed . . . Ed Thorn."

Later, as they went along the awninged walk toward the night light in the Chinaman's restaurant window, after carrying the mail sacks to the railway station, Dan was baffled. Whether he willed it or not, he knew that he couldn't hate Ed Thorn. To try and put down this feeling he scowled and looked up into Thorn's face, a full head above his own, hoping to see something reflected in it that would betray the real man, the murderer. But along the clean lines of Thorn's lean face there was nothing Dan could pin his hope on. The gray eyes looked down at him for a brief instant in an open and level regard, not in the way of a man who has a rottenness within him to hide. No coward, no one but a man with two men's share of guts, could have made that drive tonight. Everything about Thorn, the direct way in which he spoke, the sureness of his driving, even the easy grace of his tall, flat frame each time he moved, belied Dan's former belief that here was a man who had sold out his outfit, sold out the life of his guard for a price.

Dan kicked open the screen door to the Chinaman's irritably, angry at his softness. He went along the counter, ignoring three men who sat at the front end of it, and was about to take a chair at the rear when Ed Thorn's low-spoken drawl behind stopped him.

"Howdy, Frost," Thorn said.

It wasn't the words that made Dan Belden wheel around. It was the way they were spoken, softly and with a flat challenge.

Dan saw that Thorn stood behind the last place at the street end of the counter, well back from it. The man on the chair there turned slowly at the sound of Thorn's voice. He was a heavy, shapeless-framed man with sloping shoulders and thick arms and a fleshy, beard-stubbled face that had an unmistakable wickedness imprinted on it.

At sight of Thorn, a quick change wiped a measure of the arrogance from Frost's face and put a rising fear in its place. Then, over a split second's pause, Frost lunged awkwardly up from the stool with right hand streaking to his thigh. Dan, watching Ed Thorn, was amazed at the blurring swiftness with which his two hands came up and locked even with hips, a Colt in each fist. The draw was so swiftly timed that Frost was caught with gunsight not quite clear of leather.

Frost froze in a paralysis of stark fear. He let go his grip on the gun's handle. The heavy .45 fell from holster to the floor with a loud thud as the two others at the counter turned and paid particular attention to keeping their hands in plain sight.

Then Frost was saying hoarsely: "Don't, Ed. I swear to God I wasn't in with Prall on that deal."

Ed Thorn's two thumbs drew back the hammers of his twin guns. He eyed the pair with Frost and drawled flatly: "Talk, Ben. Where's Bill Prall?"

"Haven't seen him in months, Ed. I quit him cold the day after Bob Hunter's inquest."

"Because you were too honest to back his forked play?" Ed said in mock solemnity.

"That's a fact, Ed," Frost insisted, his face gone a pasty yellow beneath its tan.

In the short interval of silence that followed, Dan Belden all at once remembered something he'd been trying to put his finger on these past few seconds, ever since he'd first heard Ben Frost's voice. He walked the length of the counter until he stood alongside Ed Thorn, eyeing Frost belligerently, saying: "Three nights ago you and another ranny stopped my stage at Mile High Gulch. You went through the boot while your partner held a gun on me. When you found the boot empty, you were so damned riled you shot me just to square things." Dan's hand came up to his wounded shoulder. "You gave me this bum arm. Thorn, he's one of the gang that's been houndin' the trails since the camp opened."

Frost's face took on an ugly look. He had opened his mouth to speak, when Ed Thorn interrupted: "Dan, is there a sheriff or a marshal handy?"

Dan was quick to catch his meaning. He started for the door, saying as he went out: "It'll take me less'n five minutes to get him."

Dan found Sheriff John Parker asleep on the cot in his office at the jail. While Parker was pulling on his trousers and boots, Dan told his story of the stage hold-up three nights ago and of tonight recognizing Frost as the man who had shot him. Back at the restaurant again with the law man, he found Ed Thorn occupying the seat near the front window, a gun at his elbow on the counter, and Ben Frost sitting sullenly silent midway the length of the room. The other pair of men was gone. Back near the kitchen the Chinaman who owned the place was staring wide-eyed at his two customers.

"This him?" Parker said as he strode up to Frost. Catching Dan Belden's nod, he expertly flicked a heavy pair of handcuffs on Frost's wrists, intoning levelly: "You're under arrest for robbery and attempted murder, stranger. Come along." He took Frost roughly by the arm and pushed him toward the front door.

Frost jerked his arm from the law man's grasp when he was alongside Ed Thorn. He faced Thorn squarely, face set in a down-lipped sneer. "You'll hear more from me, friend Ed," his voice grated. "The jail hasn't been built in this tank town that'll hold me. I've got some friends who'll be glad to know where they can find you."

"Bill Prall one of 'em, Ben?"

Frost clamped his jaw shut, turned with a jerk, and went out the door. In five more seconds the sound of his and the law man's boot tread had faded out in the night's stillness downstreet.

Ed gave Dan Belden a long look. "Sounded like he meant that."

Dan shrugged, took the seat next to Thorn, and called the frightened Chinaman from his kitchen to draw them two steaming cups of black coffee. Belden ordered a wedge of pie, Thorn a plate of doughnuts, and for long minutes they ate and drank in silence.

At length, Dan Belden said lifelessly: "Well, I reckon you'll be wantin' to take the morning train out." He shifted so that he could reach into his trouser pocket. "Tom pays twenty dollars a trip. You've earned it." He took a wallet from the pocket, awkwardly thumbed out several bills, and laid them on the counter.

Ed Thorn ignored the money. He got a second cup of coffee and spent half a minute stirring a scant half teaspoonful of sugar into it before he said: "How much has Tom Hunter staked on this thing?"

"Everything he's got in the world."

Ed's sharp-planed face took on the hint of a frown. "Why? That camp up there doesn't amount to much."

"No?" Dan Belden chuckled dryly. "Wait'll the rainy season's over. Wait'll those Eastern soft-boots find out how much dust is being taken out. It's a pan and rocker diggin's now, but six months will see it booming like Silverton did, maybe bigger. Then the mail contract will amount to something. They'll put in a good road, bring in the law. The line that hauls in mail and passengers will make a cleanin'."

Ed Thorn's frown deepened. "Do you need the law up there?"

"You know how I got this, don't you?" Dan raised his good hand to his bad shoulder. "The stage has been held up before. Not only that, but in the past two weeks half a dozen claim owners have been beat up bad and their pokes emptied. You could fill ten county jails with the hardcases hangin' out up at Ledge.

It's getting so bad they're afraid to ship their winter's take in gold out for fear the stage will be raided. They're afraid to keep their dust around their camps for fear they'll be dry-gulched for it. Pretty soon they'll make a try at gettin' the whole mess down here to the bank. The day they do that, we'll dig some new graves."

Ed Thorn fell into a stolid silence. They ordered their third cups of coffee and had half finished them before Thorn spoke again. He asked abruptly: "Can Hunter get another driver for his next run?"

"Sure," Dan answered in biting sarcasm. "Hundreds of 'em. He can pick any man off the street and put him behind two teams and have him run a Concord down here any day of the week. Especially after this storm. It's smoothed out that trail so damn' well a woman could wheel a baby carriage over it without wakin' her offspring."

"How about you doin' Hunter's driving?"

"What with? My feet? Yeah. My arm'll be well day after tomorrow. Bullet holes heal up real quick."

"Let's put our cards on the table, Dan," Ed said, turning to eye Belden squarely. "Tom Hunter's in bad shape, if keeping his schedule means getting his contract. I want to help him, although you wouldn't understand why.

Half an hour ago I'd have told you and Hunter to go to hell, even if you'd gone on your knees and begged me to hire out to him. You tried to mash my head in with a chair and you pulled a gun on me because my name's Ed Thorn. But I'll forget that, providin' you handle Hunter and the girl and keep them from going at me every time they set eyes on me. I'll do Hunter's driving as long as he needs me. But get this. I'm doing it for my own reasons."

Dan jerked his head toward the door. "Because of the hardcase the sheriff took out of here?"

"Maybe."

"You think this Bill Prall is in the country?"

"Ben Frost was Prall's right bower up in Montana."

Dan Belden's expression turned serious. All the animosity drained out of him. He met Thorn's glance with a narrow-lidded and calculating one, plainly studying his man. At length he muttered an oath under his breath, saying: "I wish to hell I knew."

"Knew what?"

"What really happened up in Montana."

"You probably never will." Ed Thorn's glance went back to his coffee cup.

"You know any good reason why we should believe your story when the whole damned

156

country believes the other?"

Ed Thorn shook his head.

"What I can't figure is why the hell you'll stick here, with everything you got against you."

"I said I had my own reasons."

Dan let out a long sigh, glowered at the Chinaman sitting dozing at the far end of the counter. Suddenly he bellowed: "Louie, you lazy sidewinder! Draw me some more of this lye-water you peddle for coffee."

CHAPTER THREE

In the next week, Ed made two more trips down from Ledge to Plainsville, driving the buckboard. These two were made alone and by daylight, with the trail improved each time. Ledge citizens, cut off from the outside except for the trail, formed a voluntary crew that worked the trail from above while several Plainsville merchants, with an eye to business, hired men to do pick and shovel work below. Ed's third trip down saw him working the ribbons of a two-team light Concord. That return trip lasted well into the night with a full load of light freight and passengers and two extra teams in harness.

Not once in that week had Ed set eyes on Tom Hunter, and only once did he get a glimpse of the stage owner's daughter. But at the end of that third trip, going into the office from the barn toward midnight, expecting to find Dan Belden alone sleeping on his cot, he found the lamp lighted behind the drawn shade and Nan Hunter seated at the desk.

Belden, sitting on his cot and hunkered back to the wall, was sucking on a stem-chewed cob pipe.

The girl turned at the sound of the rear door opening. When she saw who it was, a little of the color drained from her face. But an instant later her head tilted up proudly and the hint of a forced smile softened her look.

"A good trip?" she asked pleasantly.

Ed pulled a roll of bills from a trouser pocket and stepped across to lay it on the desk. "Six passengers at a dollar a mile. Four hundred and fifty pounds of freight. Three hundred and ten dollars. Better count it."

She flushed under the subtle sting of his last words, picked up the money, and dropped it into the drawer without comment. Then she turned to look at Belden, and some understanding passed between them, for a moment later Dan was saying: "We got a problem on our hands, Thorn. See if you can help. Today, while you were gone, two claim owners were held up in broad daylight at their diggin's. One lost sixty-four ounces of dust. The other wouldn't tell where his poke was hid. So they shot him through the back. He was buried this afternoon."

Ed nodded. "The stable boy told me about it. Here's something else. Last night a bunch broke Ben Frost out of the Plainsville jail."

The look on Dan's face tightened. "He said the jail couldn't hold him." For a long moment he sat absent-mindedly sucking at his cold pipe. Then, raising his head to look at Ed, he said: "We've got a job ahead of us, Thorn. This afternoon there was a meetin' at the saloon. It was agreed that it'd be safer for everyone if all the gold in camp was put in a safe spot. It's across there now, in the saloon safe, with four guards with scatter-guns watchin' it."

"What's the job?" Ed asked.

"To get it down to the bank in Plainsville."

"Tonight?"

Belden shook his head. "No. They ain't decided yet. But it'll be soon, and we'll be travelin' under heavy guard. You're to do the drivin'."

Ed could feel the hot flush that came to his face. Except for time and place, this might be the day eight months ago when Bill Prall had put to him a similar proposition to transfer the load of bullion from a smelter safely to the vault of an express car on a railway siding seventy miles out across the Montana plains. Both Nan and Belden must have read the look on his face and caught the resemblance of the two situations, for they were kind enough to look away and let him get a hold on himself.

After several seconds, he said: "Name the day and we'll get it out."

"I thought I'd tell you . . . was all," Dan Belden said. He reached over, knocked out his pipe on the heel of his boot, and added: "Time to turn in, Nan. You'd better get on across to the hotel."

The girl got up from her chair and pulled down the shutter of the desk, locking it. She had turned away from the chair, about to go to the door, when on impulse she looked back over her shoulder at Ed and said: "Coming?"

He nodded, said — "So long, Dan." — and went to the door, holding it open for the girl.

They turned upstreet along the walk and were almost even with the flimsy frame outline of the hotel that sat across the street before either of them spoke. It was Nan who said: "Are you tired? Because if you aren't, I'd like to walk on up the cañon. Between Dad's cigars and Dan's pipe, I diet pretty much on stale air back there at the office."

As she spoke, she looked up at him and smiled in a way that was hard for him to believe, accustomed as he was to thinking how she and her father resented him. High over the towering peaks to the west, at the head of the cañon, the broad arc of a moon on the quarter gave a soft light that clearly brought out the serene beauty of the girl's face. That

161

smile, along with the unspoken trust that lay in her words, did something to Ed Thorn he hadn't thought possible. All the bitterness and hate of these past months were forgotten in an instant. Here was a girl, one who had been in his thoughts more than he'd even admitted to himself, going out of her way to be friendly. Not only that, but this girl was the sister of a man whose death he had been held responsible for.

Belief that his hearing hadn't deceived him was slow in coming, so slow that he couldn't help saying: "You're sure you . . . ?"

That was as far as he got, for she reached up and gently put her hand across his mouth. "Let's not talk about it, Ed," she said softly. "Later, sometime, I'll tell you why I can't hate you, why I know you did everything you could for Bob."

Soon they were beyond the walks that fronted the few stores at the town's center. Then they were past the limits of the dirt path that ran before the disorderly array of tents and tar paper shacks at the edge of town. As the unevenness of the ground took them over steeply climbing stretches, Nan took his arm in a way that was at once natural without being intimate.

The pressure of her hand on his arm stirred within him a longing he had never felt before, a longing to get his feet on certain ground, to start living a sure life. It was a tonic he had long needed, a stabilizing influence he had lost sight of, this hope for the future. Until now he had lived day by day, looking no further ahead than the next. Now, subtly, his hopes were building up, and it was inevitable that they should include this girl.

He was scarcely aware of the moment she started speaking, so strong were his own inward thoughts. But soon he found himself listening to the pleasant lilt of her musical voice, understanding that she was talking about her brother, of days long past when Tom Hunter had been a moderately wealthy man, loving his wife, making his life the building of a good home and the raising of his children. Then, three years ago, a second summer's drought on a cattle range in upper New Mexico had wiped out Tom Hunter's business, banking, along with many other businesses of the small community supported by the cattle industry. Nan's mother had died from heartbreak at seeing her husband dragged down. Bob had taken out on his own, in a young man's way of finding his own life and independence. Nan had stayed with her father, helped him accumulate the scant funds that finally were invested in a few horses and two discarded stagecoaches, one of them the Concord Ed had today wheeled down to Plainsville and back.

"So here we are, making a second try," the girl ended by saying. They had stopped in an open glade in the timber, and in the moonlight Ed could look down into her face and see and feel the strange intensity that had taken her. "It's a new beginning, a greater one than he had before. And, Ed, we're going to see that he doesn't fail."

"We?" he asked, and caught her slow nod.

All at once he had the impulse to take her in his arms, to tilt her chin up and kiss her lips. But with that impulse came a strength of will that locked his arms to his sides. He didn't even speak, not trusting his voice before the riot of emotion that was in him.

She must have read that battle between will and impulse on his face. For she said softly, in a voice barely above a whisper: "There'll be other times, Ed." A tenderness was in her glance as she turned away, one that accomplished an unspoken understanding between them.

The walk back down the cañon to the town ended too shortly for Ed. They were silent, each seeming not to want to break the spell by turning to the futility of words. He left her at the door of the hotel, saying — "I'll see that everything's right at the barn before I turn

164

in." — knowing that, if he went to his room, he would be awake and find the walls too confining for his thoughts.

He watched her go across the hotel verandah and in the door, then walked slowly along the street, his mind idly turning back to relive the past hour. Each look of Nan's, each tone of her voice was graven indelibly on his memory. In one short hour his life had changed, had somehow straightened out of its futile and aimless wandering.

These were the things going through his mind when a sharp-edged voice spoke its one word out of the passageway alongside the saloon: "Ed."

Instantly his long body was cocked to a sure wariness. He turned slowly to face the passageway, the fingers of his right hand already bending for the snatch that would clear his gun from its sheath.

Then, in that same muted undertone as before, the voice spoke again: "I'm lookin' at you over my sights, Ed. Keep your hands clear and step in here."

Ed was quick to see that it was at least ten feet to either side of him to the cover of the passageway's walls. While he covered that ten feet, Bill Prall could empty the gun into him. So, deliberately and unhurriedly, he turned into the cobalt blackness of the passageway.

165

He had barely moved abreast of the buildings to either side before someone stepped in behind him and lifted his pair of .45 Colts from the holsters.

"That's better," Bill Prall's voice said softly. "Follow me on back here, Ed. We have some talkin' to get off our chests."

At the end of the passageway was the littered narrow yard that ran behind the saloon. Along its far edge was the outline of a shed. Ed made out Bill Prall's high, thin shape as it crossed the strip of open yard toward the shed. When he himself was clear of the passageway, he looked back over his shoulder to see who followed him. It was Ben Frost. Ben's big hands fisted a pair of guns, and, as he caught Ed's backward glance, his thick, ugly face took on a sneering smile plainly visible in the moonlight.

"Like it, Ed?" he rasped, and hefted his right-hand gun in a signal that Ed should go on.

When Ed came up to the shed, it was to find Prall hunkered down on his heels, leaning back against the wall on the lighted side of the small building. Prall's wide, flat-crowned Stetson was pushed back onto his head so that it revealed his narrow, high forehead and long, cadaverous face. A short, square-clipped beard accentuated the length of his face. The smile of his thin lips was mocking, almost satanical, and made sharper by the thin line of a mustache. He said: "Make yourself comfortable while we chew the fat." He gave Ben Frost a short nod. "Over there, Ben, and get plenty far away. Cover him and don't try to listen too hard."

Frost cleared his throat in a plain sign of anger, saying belligerently: "I don't get this, Bill. Either I'm in on it, or I'm not."

"Want to pull out?" Prall drawled.

Frost waited there a moment, barely out of Ed's reach, before he sullenly backed away across the yard and took up his stand twenty feet away, leaning against the waist-high, thick stump of a cedar, guns ready.

"Ben was always a little careless of his tongue," Prall explained in a soft voice Frost couldn't hear. "What I have to say won't bear repeatin' over a bottle of whisky." He looked up at Ed, and his flat chest moved in a silent yet hearty laugh. "Didn't expect to find me here, did you?"

Ed said: "Sooner or later Ben will get careless. When he does, you'd better begin sayin' your prayers, Prall."

Bill Prall's smile held. "Still riled about the deal up in Montana? Hell, forget it! I had to make a start somewhere. That was it. Now I can give you your start."

"You have a habit of helpin' people."

"Look at it this way, then," Prall went on, unruffled by the sarcasm. "There's a big job here. I can't handle it alone. But I can with your help. I cut you in on a third share. It'll amount to something like fifteen thousand. How does it sound?"

"Like I'd expect it to. Rotten."

"Easy, Ed. You aren't callin' the deal right now." Prall paused long enough to let his words carry their weight. Then: "You can't tell me you aren't fed up on the pushin' around they've given you since you left Montana. Get wise to yourself. Make a cleanin' and take what you can and move on to a new country where you can live easy and hold your head up. Sure, I framed that Montana deal on you. What of it? Now I'm makin' up for it."

The live anger within Ed was settling before a cold and calculating nervelessness. Here was the man he hated above all others, the man who had dragged down his name, made a wreck of his life. Yet in the face of all that, Ed was aware of other things. Prall had somehow learned what had happened these past eight months, had learned of the long downgrade that had only a week ago brought Ed to this boom town resolving that, if this last chance turned against him, he had no choice but to accept an end to honest living. He had gone down that far, far enough to begin thinking of the Owlhoot as the only way out. Prall knew that and was banking on it now, banking on the fact that Ed had been kicked around enough to be willing to listen to a plan for making easy money and paying back a world that wouldn't have him.

What Prall didn't know was that tonight something had happened to make up for the endless torture of these past months. But why not play along with Prall, acting the part of the man whose bitterness against the world had turned him into a prospective lawbreaker? Sooner or later he'd have the chance to even things with Prall.

No sooner had the thought come to Ed than he was saying: "I'd trust you about as far as I could toss an anvil. But right now I'd bed down with a rattler if he'd make me a good partner. Get it off your chest, Bill. I'll listen."

"That's better." Prall leaned back against the side of the shed, took out tobacco and papers, and built a smoke. When he'd finished, he passed the makings on across to Ed, who performed the same ritual in silence.

"Better understand one thing straight off," Prall said, when he'd lit his cigarette. "There isn't a trace of proof against me on what happened in Montana, so don't think you can turn me in for it. Ben doesn't even know all that happened. Maybe you do, but it's your word against mine, and your word doesn't count for a damn. I stayed on the job in Montana three months after you'd gone. I quit the job on my own. I have a good name. I'm up here on legitimate business. So don't try a double-cross."

"I'd double-cross you the first chance you gave me, Bill," Ed said evenly. "You ought to know that."

Once again came that dry, almost sound-less laugh of Prall's. "You're damn' right I know it. But you won't get the chance. Until we busted Ben out of that jail below, I didn't have anything in mind but shaking down these claim owners. Now that you're here, things stack up different."

"How?"

"There's gold going out soon. You're the only driver Hunter has to take it."

In the following silence, Ed saw what was coming. He said tonelessly: "We take the gold, split it, and clear out?"

Prall nodded. "Exactly. A third for me, a third for you, the other third to be split six ways between my men. Ben's the only one of the six who knows me, and I've got some-thing on Ben that'll keep his mouth shut till he dies. Find a hole in the set-up and you're a better man than I am."

"I could give you away."

"You could, but you won't. Fifteen thousand is a hell of a big stake to a man who can't keep a job beyond the time his name's known."

Ed smiled wryly, and said in a grudging way: "You think of everything, Prall."

"I make it my business to. Here's the layout. That gold can't stay there under guard in the saloon more than a couple of days. The owners won't let it. My hunch is that you'll be taking it down your next trip, maybe tomorrow even. They'll have enough scatter-guns to stop an army. There's where you come in."

"Don't tell me you'll be one of the guards," Ed said in open sarcasm.

Prall shook his head. "When it happens, I'll probably be in the saloon here having a drink of the four-year-old bourbon I turned over to the bartender as my own special bottle. There'll be nothing to connect me to what happens."

"You said that once before. Get on with it."

"Six miles down the cañon," Prall began, in a voice barely above a whisper so that Ben Frost couldn't overhear, "the trail takes a hairpin turn to the left. The ledge there is narrow, barely wide enough for a team. There's a straight-down drop-off better than a hundred feet. Inside the turn, the wall goes up for fifty feet so sudden a goat couldn't climb it. Remember the place?"

Ed nodded.

"At that turn, you're on the inside. The stage is loaded with guards inside and out. You hit the turn at a pretty fair speed, with brakes set. Supposin' you were to give a jerk on the reins and pull your teams sharp toward the drop-off?"

Ed's face gathered in a frown, then eased into a cold smile. "A jughead don't have much sense. One of them'd step out over the drop-off."

"With one horse down the others would be dragged over, wouldn't they? They'd take stage, gold, guards, everything with them."

"Includin' me."

Prall shook his head. "I've already said you'd be on the inside of the turn. You'd jump."

"All right, I'd jump. What then?"

"Maybe a couple of the guards would jump, too. But with three of my men forted up in the rocks above the turn with rifles, and with three more below to cut down any cripples that live, we could handle twenty men, couldn't we?"

"You could handle me, too."

Prall smiled. "I knew you'd think of that.

Here's my guarantee that I'm playing square with you. There's an overhang of rock right around the turn. From there, you can't be cut down from above, and, if you jump off with a rifle, you'll have those below covered. You're to take charge then, to see that every man on that stage is wiped out and that my men don't double-cross me. They'll be instructed to rope the box with the gold in it on a lead pony and to leave another pony for you. Then they're to go down the cañon and keep in plain sight until you've climbed down to the horses. You're to ride over to them, take their guns away, and then let them lead you up to the hide-out. I meet you there that night, and we make the split. From then on it'll be up to you to take care of your own hide."

Prall flicked his smoke away so that the burning stub made a high arc out into the moonlit, cluttered yard and struck the ground in a shower of sparks. "How does it sound?"

"Like you could be held on about fifteen counts of murder."

"You'll soon learn to live with your conscience," Prall said. "It isn't hard." He tilted his head up and surveyed Ed directly. "Are you in on it?"

"Why not?" Ed shrugged. "I'll never save fifteen thousand at driver's wages."

"Come on over, Ben," Prall called, getting to his feet.

He had barely straightened when Ed, seeing that Ben had sheathed his guns, made a sudden lunge. His hands streaked out and pinned Prall's arms to his sides. He lifted Prall bodily before him as a shield as Ben all at once stopped and streaked his hands for his guns. Then, locking one arm around Prall and spreading his feet to avoid Prall's back-slashing spurs as he struggled to free himself, Ed reached down and took the gun from Prall's right-hand holster. Ben, both guns lined, hesitated to shoot.

Ed rammed the gun in Prall's back, saying softly: "Tell Ben to be good. Tell him what to do with his irons."

Prall called in a voice edged with cold hate: "Drop 'em, Ben!"

The burly gunman hesitated only a second before he let his guns fall to the ground. With a lurch, Ed let go of Prall, swinging him so viciously that Prall fell on hands and knees. He moved the short-barreled .45 in a tight arc that covered both men, saying: "It'd take two shots from this hogleg to frame it to look like you'd shot it out between you, Prall. Can you think of any reason I shouldn't do it?"

Prall, coming erect, said hoarsely: "Ed, for

God's sake! You're throwing away fifteen thousand in gold!"

"I could swing it on my own."

Prall quickly shook his head. "You couldn't. You need me and my men."

"And you need me," Ed drawled. He abruptly tossed the gun across so that it fell to the ground at Prall's feet. "Which is the best proof I know of why we shouldn't cut each other's throats."

Prall stood stock still for a long moment before he stooped and picked up the .45. He made a motion that stayed Ben Frost's gesture of picking up the other pair of weapons, saying: "Easy, Ben." Then, to Ed: "What was the idea of that play?"

"Just to let you know that you don't think of everything, Prall."

Chapter Four

On his way from the hotel to the stage office next morning, Ed saw the crowd gathered before the saloon and knew that today was the day the gold was being shipped. The ringing sounds of pick and shovel, from upcañon, sounds he'd long ago learned to recognize, weren't breaking the stillness of the cool mountain air today. The size of the crowd spilling out across the plank walk and into the street between saloon and stage station told him that every man in Ledge was gathered there, the majority of them there out of an instinct to protect their property represented by the gold in the saloon safe.

He swung obliquely out across the street at the margins of the crowd toward the office. A smaller group was gathered before the door here. Men stepped respectfully aside to let him to the door, for everyone had heard of the night's drive a week ago in the storm, and he had tacitly gone along with the Deerfoot's trust in him.

Inside, he found Nan, Tom Hunter, and Dan Belden standing by the desk, talking. Tom Hunter glowered at him, Nan and Belden both spoke politely, and their talk went on, ignoring him at first but finally including him as Nan said: "You'll have ten men riding guard today, Ed. The gold's. . . ."

"Ed?" her father cut in sharply, eyeing her in anger. "Since when are you calling your brother's killer by his first name?"

"Dad," the girl said mildly, "we might as well have this out now. Ed Thorn didn't kill Bob. I know it, and you must believe it. Ed was framed. Look at him! Does he look like a man who'd sell out his friends?"

Ed could see the gathering anger in Tom Hunter's face, and knew that the stage owner was ready to explode with fury. So he said sharply: "Let's forget that business. Here's something you all ought to know if the gold's headed down today." He went on briefly but concisely, telling of his meeting with Bill Prall last night, of the deal he had made with Prall for taking the gold.

When he'd finished, there was a tense ten-second silence, broken finally by Tom Hunter's suspicious: "How do we know you're telling the truth?"

"What point would there be in my not telling it?"

Ed's answer apparently satisfied Hunter, for the stage owner pulled his swivel chair to the desk and sat down wearily in it, his anger toward Ed forgotten as he said: "Now what?"

Ed turned to Belden. "Dan, see if I've got this straight. Half a mile this side of that turn there's a low pass that cuts through to the trail beyond the bend. Right?"

Dan frowned a moment in thought, then nodded.

Ed went on: "How far would you say it was through that pass to the trail after it makes the turn?"

"Quarter of a mile maybe. But, hell, you couldn't drive it."

"No, but half the guards we take along could walk it, couldn't they? And the rest could take to the bottom of the cañon and work up on Prall's men below."

Tom Hunter sat straighter in his chair. "See here, Thorn, where do you stand in this? What's this getting you?"

"I'm not sure. It may get me proof against Prall on that Montana job."

"What about the gold?" Nan asked worriedly.

"Leave the gold here," Ed told her. "Have it brought across here to the office before we start. Let only the men who are to ride guard come into the office. No one else should know. We'll fill the box with sand and leave a couple of men here with the gold until we've finished the thing. Down the trail, we can split our men, send half of them to the pinnacle above the bend, the rest below to take care of Prall's men there. Hunter, you'll stay behind to take Prall. He bragged that he'd be over in the saloon having a drink when the play came off. Wait half an hour or so and go over and stick a gun in his back. He's tall, with a spade beard and mustache. You'll know him."

Hunter nodded after a moment. "But what proof have we against him?"

"I'll make Ben Frost talk. We'll give him his choice, either to talk or hang. He'll talk."

Hunter solemnly struck the desk top with his open palm, looking up at Ed and saying levelly: "Damned if I know why, but I'm wishin' you luck, Thorn. Maybe I'm goin' soft, but it'd please me to know it was a stranger and not you that cost me my son."

"Dad, I knew you'd see it!" Nan cried.

Hunter shook his head. "Not yet, I don't. But I'm willing to have it proven. Nan, go across with Thorn and find Sam Shipley. Tell him to get those guards in here. We start in an hour. We'll load out back, where the whole town can't see."

Bill Prall was one of the crowd in front of

179

the Nugget Saloon. Ben Frost was in at the bar, waiting for the word that would send him down the cañon to meet the five other men and place them, as arranged, below and above the bend where Ed Thorn was to drive the stage over the rim.

Prall saw Ed come out of the hotel and go across to the stage station. His cold glance followed Ed every step of the way, and the fact that he had an inward doubt would have been obvious to an onlooker. For ten minutes after Ed had disappeared inside the stage office, Prall leaned idly against the wall of the assayer's office next to the saloon, relishing the taste of his after-breakfast cigar.

He was standing there, listening idly to the talk of the men at the near edge of the crowd, when he saw Ed Thorn and Nan Hunter come out of the stage station door. They started across the street toward the saloon, and Prall's glance observed them critically. His eyes narrowed a trifle as he saw the girl put her arm through Thorn's, and, when Nan smiled up at Ed and said something to him, Prall's long face took on a tight, calculating scowl. He caught Ed's down tilt of the head in answering the girl, caught, too, the readable interest written on Ed's face and in his smile.

That exchange of glances between Ed and Nan did something to Bill Prall. It erased the pleasantness from his black eyes, turned their expression hard as rimrock. A less sharp observer than Prall could easily have read the look he'd seen on Nan Hunter's face. She was in love with this Ed Thorn, and, unless Prall was far wrong, Ed returned that feeling.

For a full minute after the call rang out for the guards, after ten men with shotguns followed Ed and Nan back to the stage office, Bill Prall stood there considering what he had seen. At the end of that interval a vague, shadowy smile played across his thin face. He took a last full drag at the cigar, inhaling deeply, then he tossed the generous unused length of the Havana into the street and pushed his way into the crowd before the saloon's swing doors.

Inside, he made his way to the bar, standing alongside Ben Frost. He ignored Frost and called for a drink from his private bottle. Then, when the apron had stepped out of hearing, Prall spoke in a low voice without lifting his head from regarding his shot glass. Ben Frost, listening, was at first surprised, then puzzled. He put two low-worded questions, the last salty with an oath, and afterward listened with a rock-like set to his face as Prall kept talking. Then, shortly, he left the bar and sauntered out the door up front. Prall downed his drink and went across the room to look on at a game of stud.

For a quarter hour nothing happened. Then the mutter of voices from the crowd outside rose a full tone in pitch, and the ten gold guards came in through the doors and walked on back to the huge black safe standing at the rear wall and flanked on each side by a man with a shotgun under his arm. The guards ringed the safe, and one of them stooped and worked the combination.

When the guards filed out half a minute later, each of them was stooped under the weight of a small heavy burlap sack bulging unevenly with the smaller rawhide pokes it contained. Prall's eyes followed the progress of each of those sacks from safe to door, and there was a light of greed in his look and a shadowed smile on his face.

In the stage office, Tom Hunter held the door open as the guards entered. He closed it after the last man and crossed the room to watch the last of the sacks being pushed under Dan Belden's cot. One change had been made in their plans; the stage was to be loaded on the street, in full sight of all. As Hunter heard the rattle of the Concord's doubletree chains sound out from the back, he called sharply: "Hurry it up! Get those poles through the straps and four of you lug the box out."

182

A solid, brass-bound trunk filled with sand and slung by harness straps from two poles was carried out onto the walk, ringed by the guards who carried their Greeners at the ready, fingers on the triggers. The Concord, Ed at the ribbons, rolled out of the wide passageway alongside the station from the barn and corrals. Tom Hunter bellowed an impressive warning to the nearest watchers along the walk, ordering them to keep back. The brass-bound trunk was lifted in the door, its weight making the stage settle lower on the thoroughbraces. Four guards went in the door after it, poking their shotguns menacingly out the lowered windows to either side. Four more climbed to the top, one sitting alongside Ed, two on the roof, another standing in the rear boot. Dan Belden swung up to sit between Ed and the guard on the seat. As Hunter gave the order to roll, the two remaining guards swung aboard the steps.

The Concord lurched as the Morgans took Ed's signal through the reins. The teams lunged into the harness, gathering speed slowly under the stage's heavy weight. Finally the coach rolled to the center of the street, the teams at a trot. It was an impressive sight, one that called forth a cheer from the crowd on either side. Before the town's crude shacks fell away behind, the Morgans were at a slow canter, kicking up a light fog of dust from the trail that had a week ago been fetlock-deep in mud.

Dan Belden was nervous as a cat for a reason he couldn't define. He shot a sideward look at Ed, realizing that the driver of this heavily loaded stage had his hands full keeping to the rough trail. "Better take it easy," he cautioned, knowing as he spoke that there was nothing he could say that would improve Ed's driving.

In the next three miles, Ed time and again stood erect, boot on the brake, hands busy with the lines that made the three teams of Morgans respond instantly to his will. No word was spoken among the guards, who were keyed up to what was coming. Finally, half a mile short of the bend where the ambush was laid, Ed booted home the brake on a slight upgrade and brought the Morgans to a slow stop.

The guards got down and gathered on the trail near the front wheel hub on Ed's side. Their leader divided them into two groups. Ed called down a last word: "I want one man taken alive. He's big and wears a pair of irons. You'll be able to tell him by the conch hatband on a gray hat. Save him for me." He was speaking of Ben Frost.

He and Dan Belden watched the guards

split and go their different ways, the first group of five men climbing off the trail through a wide, precipitous notch that went stiffly upward at right angles. The remaining five men worked their way down the shelving side of the cañon to its bottom, barely twenty feet below at this point. Soon all ten men had passed out of sight, and, except for an occasional fly-prompted hoof stomp from the horses, the cañon's silence was complete and somehow ominous.

Dan Belden took out his cob pipe and filled it; his right arm, out of its sling now, moved with awkward stiffness. As he lit his smoke, he said: "There ain't one man in a hundred knows how to smoke a pipe. They go at it too fast. Takes twenty minutes to smoke one down properly, and the man that lets it go out on him meantime loses the best of the weed's taste."

He took two slow puffs and leaned out and spat expertly into the trail, and Ed understood that Belden meant to smoke out the pipe before they moved on, thus making sure that the guards were in position.

Something was worrying Ed, and he worded it a few minutes later: "Dan, I wouldn't give a Mex *peso* for my chances when I strike that bend. You'd better wait here until it's over."

"Like hell I will," the driver blustered. He smacked with an open palm the stock of the rifle alongside him on the seat. "I'm gettin' in at least one shot. Hell, I ain't earned my salt around here for nigh onto ten days. Tom'll be firin' me next thing you know."

Ed knew then that it was useless to try and change Belden's mind. They sat wordlessly for five minutes longer, for ten. Finally Belden shifted his shoulders nervously and said: "I'm a poor hand at fancy words, Thorn. But I'd like you to know that my feelin's are about the same as Nan's. About what you've done for us, I mean. Tom's ornery . . . has a right to be. But he'll come around, too, in the end. There's a place here for you as long as you want to stay, regardless of what comes of this business today."

"Thanks, Dan," Ed said. Then he unwound the reins from the brake arm, saying impatiently: "It's time we were rollin'."

Belden looked down at his pipe critically, tested it with a long inhalation. "Reckon you're right," he agreed, and knocked the dottle from it and put it in his shirt pocket.

They started on a few moments later, the Morgans straining against the harness for the long, stiff upgrade that lay ahead. They made the crest, and now the trail followed a high ledge that kept to the winding contours of the sheer wall, nearly a hundred feet above the cañon bottom. Shortly, they could see ahead the abrupt hairpin turning the cañon made in switching back on itself.

Ed found it hard not to look upward toward the rim, to the spot where he knew Prall's men were waiting, probably with rifles already lined. He said — "Be ready to jump if they open up, Dan!" — as he reined the teams into the beginning of the turn. They pulled abreast of the wall's jutting ending, the Morgans swinging on around it and hugging the wall. Now Ed reached for his whip and snaked it out in an exploding *crack* that sent the teams at a lunge against harness. The stage rounded the bend in a skid, tilting immediately into the slight downgrade on the straight of way beyond, horses at a run.

They went on, twenty yards, thirty, and still no shots came from above or below. A hundred yards on, Ed eased back on the ribbons and thrust tight the brake, hackles rising along his neck as his wariness gave way to uncertainty. The Concord lurched to a slow stop. Ed wound the ribbons around the brake arm and, only then, looked at Dan Belden. The oldster's face was a study in bewilderment. They both looked upward to the rim. There, as they stared upward, stood a man, one of their own guards, waving his arms and

187

shouting: "No one here!"

Belden's glance came down to meet Ed's. "What'd he say?" Then, because he didn't believe it, Belden looked upward again and bawled: "Look again, damn it!" He climbed down from the seat and started restlessly pacing the trail alongside the Concord.

Ed stayed where he was, a little shaken at the implications of what had been said. Soon he heard sounds above him and looked up to see the five guards picking their way down over the ledges toward the trail.

"Here come the rest," Dan said, pointing below. The other guards were in sight now, well below the point where the stage stood, climbing upward to the trail from the bottom of the cañon.

Belden's glance met Ed's. There was doubt in it, only that. "What do you figure happened?" he asked in a solemn voice.

As if in answer to his question, the breeze that gentled down the cañon brought to them at that very instant the distance-muted echo of gunfire. That sound brought Ed rigid in the grip of a slow paralysis, made Dan Belden whip his head around and cock it to hear better.

"Hell, it's comin' from up there . . . from town," Belden said hoarsely.

Ed was already kicking off the brake, pulling

the lead team over to the edge of the drop-off. He used all the roadway he could and then backed the Morgans until the Concord's rear wheels grated against the cliff face. He repeated the maneuver, and, by the time the guards from the rim had made the trail, the stage was half turned. The guards had heard the guns from above and now ran over to the Concord and helped without a word. Four men lifted and hauled the stage's rear around; two more took the bits of the lead team and helped Ed complete the turn. It was done as the five from below came running up along the trail.

The guards piled into the stage as Dan Belden swung onto the seat alongside Ed, saying curtly and in a new, unfriendly voice: "You'd damned well better burn up this trail gettin' back there!"

In that instant, Ed knew what Belden was thinking, knew that he stood accused of having decoyed the guards down here away from town while the gold remained all but unguarded. He laid his whip across the rumps of the Morgans, took the bend at a skid that put the rear wheels within a foot of the drop-off, and raced along the winding ledge. On the next downgrade he had to brake the Concord to keep it from overrunning the teams. The long two-mile pull back into the town from the cañon bottom was made at a full run with the whip cracking brutally between the ears of the swing team.

The Concord lurched into the lower end of the street, and Ed could see that men were running across it toward Tom Hunter's office. He skidded the stage to a quick stop, vaulted down off the seat, and shouldered aside a man on his way in through the station's door, hearing the guards coming close behind him.

Inside the room, he stopped short. Tom Hunter, ringed by a group of silent onlookers, sat on Dan Belden's cot at the rear of the room, elbows on knees and his shaggy head held in his hands. Eyes turned to see who had come in the door. Then, no word being spoken, men stepped back, and a lane was cleared between Ed and Tom Hunter. He could feel the presence of the guards at his back and, looking sideward, saw that Dan Belden stood off to his left. The room's rear door opened, and Nan came in. She stopped when she saw Ed, and her hand came up to her mouth.

When the stillness in the room had settled to an unbearably low pitch, Tom Hunter sensed it and raised his head. Ed saw then that the stage owner's shirt was smeared with blood under the left armpit. He forgot that a moment later as Hunter's high and thick frame came up slowly off the cot.

Hunter came toward him, brushing aside the hand of the one man who reached out to stop him. His rock-like face was set in a look of cold and bleak rage.

His booming voice intoned: "Gone, every damned ounce of it! I was alone, without a gun. And you've got the gall to come back here and face us!"

Dan Belden said: "Easy, Tom. Don't bloody your hands on him. We've got him, and there's ways of makin' him pay for what he's done."

Someone stepped in behind Ed and lifted his two guns from his holsters. The ominous silence drew out, Tom Hunter's face paling before his rage. Hunter said in a hoarse, derisive voice: "And I was beginning to think you were straight." The riot of emotion in him made him lose his grip on himself then. He stepped in and swung both fists with a force behind them that would have killed Ed had they connected with his jaw. Ed rolled aside from the first, took the other on his hunched shoulder. Then men crowded in from either side and pinned his arms and dragged Tom Hunter, fighting, away from him.

Someone near the door cried: "Get a rope!"

That shout seemed strangely to calm Tom

Hunter. He pulled his arms free from the hands that held him, booming: "No! Hold on! Listen, all of you!" He threw up his hands in a gesture that commanded immediate silence. Someone at the door rasped — "Quiet out there!" — and the angry mutter of voices from the crowd that packed the walk died out.

Hunter said ominously: "We'll save the rope. Thorn is one of a gang, and the gang will stick by him like they did the killer who was in jail in Plainsville last week. They won't leave without him. Let's give them the chance to come after him. When they do, we'll have the lot."

Into the crescendo of rising voices that was a mixture of agreement and protest, Dan Belden said: "You're takin' a long chance, Tom."

"Never mind how long it is," Tom Hunter said in stentorian tones that rose above the other voices. "We can try it. If it doesn't work out, we've still got him for the hang noose."

Ed heard all this and the wrangling that followed with only half his attention directed to it. He was looking over the heads of the men in front of him, seeing Nan Hunter still standing there at the back door, her eyes wide in an expression that was a mixture of fear and deep hurt. As Tom Hunter's deep bass once more crowded in on the other voices, Ed saw a change ride over the girl's face. Tears came to her eyes, and then they were edged with a look of defiance and loathing. He knew in that moment that she no longer believed in him, that she was with the others in their hatred for him.

Tom Hunter was saying: "We'll hold a vote of those present. All in favor of jailing Thorn and keeping him as bait for his gang, say, aye." A chorus of voices obeyed, but the "noes" were blended so strongly with them that Hunter called: "Raise your hands if you agree."

He paused a moment, counting the up-raised hands. Then: "All in favor of the rope." He counted once more, and said finally: "Thorn goes to jail."

Once more he gestured for silence against the protesting mutter of the men who didn't agree. Slowly he got the attention of all those in the room, and went on: "We don't have a jail in town. We'll make one. The assay office will do. Now here's how we'll work it. Two men will stand guard over the assay office night and day. Two aren't enough to bother Thorn's wild bunch, if they take it into their heads to bust him out. So we're invitin' just that. Another thing. Whoever's behind this may have men in that crowd out there. I know every man in here now, know that he's to be trusted. There's eighteen or twenty of us. I want the word of each man in here that he'll keep this plan to himself. Otherwise, it won't work."

He then spoke to each man in the room individually, countering a few arguments with the promise that Ed Thorn would sooner or later hang from the rafters of the new general store going up four doors below the stage station. "All we're doin' is trying to get the gold back," he said finally, and this was the argument that convinced the last few rebellious members of the gathering.

Once he had the promise of every man not to repeat a word of their plans, he gave Ed a last long look. Instead of anger, a cool smile was imprinted on his square face. "It'll be the greatest day of my life when I kick a sawhorse out from under you and watch a rope break your neck, Thorn. All I regret is that Bob won't be here to see it." Then, gruffly, as a deep emotion rode through him, he added: "Take him over to the lockup!"

Rough hands jerked Ed backward to the door. He cast a last glance at the girl and saw again the loathing in her eyes. It brought a shock to him that dulled the pain of the blows rained on him on the way across the street. The crowd, enraged over the loss of the gold, time and again broke through the aisle of men guarding him. Sticks and stones hit him in the face and body. When at last he was hurriedly pushed through the door of the assay office, his face was bleeding from a dozen cuts, one eye swollen nearly shut, and his jaw hurt with each flexing of his face muscles.

The door slammed shut behind him, and he heard the grating of the hasp as a padlock was clicked shut. "Clear the walk!" shouted one of the half dozen men who had brought him across the street. Only the menace of their guns finally forced the crowd back off the plank walk. The crowd was slow in breaking up, and for half an hour Ed had to listen to the obscene shouts and curses linked with his name.

In that interval a pair of men came to nail two thicknesses of hog wire across the room's two windows, front and back. When the thunder of their hammers died out, the street immediately in front of the small, one-room, board shack was clear and guards had been posted front and back, each wearing a pair of six-guns and cradling a double-barreled scatter-gun in his arm.

For the first time Ed took note of the details of the room. Its furnishings were scanty, a table at the center, two straight-backed chairs alongside it. A sturdy waist-high shelf ran along the back wall, and on it and along the floor beneath were arrayed carboys of acid, a long row of bottles containing chemicals, small sacks of pre-samples tagged with the names of their owners. There were a few ledgers, a tall deal file case against the wall to the right, and a folded dirty tarpaulin lying on the floor. Along the left wall was built a small brick charcoal furnace, flat-topped and with clay retorts on its top; nearby was a wide workbench with a pair of delicate balances under a glass cover centering its top.

Ed, like every other man who has lived a full and partly riotous life, had seen the inside of more than one jail. He now smiled, a trifle bitterly, at the thought that he could break out of here at any point he chose by merely ramming his shoulder through the sheathing of the wall. But this jail, unlike any other he had ever seen, held the menace of death for him. Those guards outside, probably men who had lost their share of gold today, wouldn't hesitate one instant in throwing a charge of buckshot into him if he tried a break.

He sat in one of the chairs at the table, deliberately considering how subtly Bill Prall had tricked him. It had been Prall in Montana, and now it was Prall again who knocked the props from under a life that held the promise of becoming well-ordered and full. He smiled grimly at the odds he saw against him. He had the undying hate of Bob Hunter's father; his name, known through the boom camp, had one more crime chalked up against it; this time he had betrayed not one man and a small organization but a whole community. Each man who had today lost his small or big fortune in the stealing of that gold would remember the name of Ed Thorn to his dying day with bitterness and hatred.

Added to this was the knowledge of how Dan Belden and Tom Hunter would believe that he had betrayed their trust in him. Two hours ago Tom Hunter had been on the point of forgiveness and belief in his innocence. Dan Belden had long ago had his doubt of Ed's guilt and become a true admirer of his skill at driving. All this was gone now, and two men who might have become real friends were bitter enemies.

Worst of all was what he put off remembering time and again. Nan Hunter's look of utter disgust and loathing was the hardest blow of all to bear. She would be remembering the trust she had placed in him last night, the admission she had been on the verge of making. Last night had seen the beginning of a deep and true love growing between them. Today he was nothing but the man who had deceived an unsuspecting populace by clearing the way for the theft of a winter's take in gold from a diggings that promised to rival the bigness of any the Rockies boasted.

Once again the old feeling of helplessness and frustration settled over him. Once again he became the bitter, grudging man who hated the world and what it had done to him. He realized with a deep and growing conviction that this was the end of all his finer instincts and that, if he outlived this trouble, he would become a sure recruit for the Outlaw Trail. The world would no longer have him; he wondered if he cared, and, finally, remembering Nan Hunter's look of utter detestation, he knew that he didn't.

CHAPTER FIVE

The hours of the day dragged on slowly, and, by the time the quick mountain dusk was settling along the cañon, Ed Thorn had become a hard and embittered man trying to think of a way out of this hopeless situation. His thoughts of escape were hurried by sounds that were overheard from the saloon immediately next door. The loud talk and occasional shouts came to him through the flimsy board wall of his small room, and he read in the tenor of those voices a growing mob anger.

He considered and cast aside a dozen plans of breaking clear of the assay office and the two guards posted outside. At dusk he was no further along than he'd been during his first hour here. The one undeniable fact staring him in the face, the one he couldn't figure a way around, was that two men stood outside ready to shoot him down.

Once he tried to call in the guard out front, asking for a drink of water. His only answer was a mocking laugh, then an ignoring of his

further calls. "You couldn't drink enough water to do you any good where you're headed.
Why try?" had been the guard's derisive answer. Ed knew then that no trickery, not even
bribery, would clear the way outside.

As the room's deep gloom settled into complete darkness, he heard the guard in front
call a flat challenge to someone who came
along the walk. It was Nan Hunter's voice
that answered: "I want to see Thorn. I have
his supper here."

"Sorry, miss," came the guard's reply. "My
orders was to let no one in."

"My father sent me," Nan said, her voice
carrying the faint edge of anger. "You can't
starve a man to death if you hope to hang
him."

There were several moments of silence, in
which the undertone of voices from the saloon next door drifted in to Ed. Then came
the guard's grudging assent. "All right. I'll let
you in. Wait'll I get this lantern lit."

The padlock grated on the door hasp, and
in a few more seconds the panel swung open.
Nan Hunter's slim figure was outlined by the
light of the lantern held in the guard's hand.
The guard said — "Here, take this." — and
handed the girl the lantern cautiously, stepping away from the door immediately afterward.

"I'll stay here until he's finished eating," Nan said, coming into the room carrying a lard pail in one hand, the lantern in the other. She eyed Ed a moment in silence, then turned to the man outside and said: "I'd feel better if you'd lock the door and stand at the window."

"Sure, miss. I'll blow him in two if he makes a move at you."

With a last malevolent glance in at Ed, the guard swung the door shut, locked it, and a moment later his shadow showed outside the window on the walk.

Nan set the pail on the table at the room's center, keeping the table between herself and Ed. She said: "It's beef stew. There's a spoon in there for you to eat it with." She pulled back a chair from the table and sat in it, her back to the window. Then, as Ed was reaching for the pail, she said in a voice barely above a whisper: "I want you to talk to me while you eat, loud enough so that he can hear. Talk about anything, but listen to what I have to say."

Deep within Ed there was a surging of renewed hope. Keeping his face from betraying that emotion, he took the chair at the opposite side of the table and removed the lid from the pail. Inside he found a spoon, and immediately began eating the tasty, well-seasoned stew. Looking down, he said in a low voice: "Then you're not with the others, Nan? You don't hate me?"

"I hate you more than anyone in the world," she said in a harsh, low-toned voice.

He looked up quickly and saw the same expression in her eyes as had been there that morning in her father's office. It brought a definite shock to him, plunged him once more into the depths of hopelessness.

"But I can't forget last night, that for a time I believed in you, nearly loved you," she went on. "Because of that, I can't see you die the way they've planned, at the end of a rope. I'm going to give you a chance to get away, as far away from here as horseflesh will carry you. What happens then is none of my concern. Sooner or later your past will catch up with you. You'll die by a bullet, perhaps by the rope. But, at least, I can face my conscience. I'd give even a rattler a chance to live."

Dully, no longer tasting his food, Ed went through the motions of eating. He forgot that she had asked him to make a pretense of talking for the guard's benefit. It seemed long minutes, although in reality it was scant seconds, before the girl continued in that same barely audible voice.

"I've hired a man to help me. I thought I'd get Dan, but he's taken a stage down the

202

cañon. Directly up the hill from here is a saw-mill. There are logs stacked on a shelf of ground up there, a huge pile of them. This saloon tramp I've hired is going to knock the wedges from under those logs. They'll roll down the hill and crush in the rear of this shack. It'll be your chance to get away. Take it, if you want."

"Maybe you'll be saving your father and the rest the job of hangin' me," Ed said dryly. "What's to keep those logs from comin' on through to the street?"

"They won't," she said. "Last winter one broke loose by accident and rolled down here. It caved in the back wall of this shack and knocked down that shelf." She nodded to indicate the long shelf along the wall at the rear. "So I know what I'm doing. You won't be hurt." She said this last with a touch of bitter sarcasm.

Ed dropped the spoon into the half-finished stew and pushed the pail from him, his hunger gone. "I don't suppose it'd do any good to try and tell you that I didn't have a hand in what happened today," he said. "That Prall fooled me like he did the rest of you."

She rose from her chair, took the pail from the table, and started for the door. "No, it wouldn't do you any good, Ed Thorn."

Ed shrugged his wide shoulders and

203

reached for the sack of tobacco in his shirt pocket. "What's all the fuss next door?" he queried, trying to keep his voice to a casual drawl.

"The beginnings of a lynch mob, I think," Nan said. "A buyer from a big Eastern mining outfit rode in this afternoon. He's buying up options on a few claims and giving out free drinks. Maybe you've seen what whisky can do to a few hotheads."

Ed nodded, smiling grimly. A sudden thought sobered him and made him ask: "What does this buyer look like?"

"Tall, thin, with a long face. Nicely dressed. A city man."

"Beard and mustache?" Ed asked, becoming tense.

Nan shook her head, smiling bleakly. "No. And don't try to tell me it's this Bill Prall. Dad says that more likely than not Prall's never been in this country."

Ed stepped around the table toward her, saying: "What color are his eyes, his hair?"

A tapping came at the window, and the guard outside called: "Back away from her, Thorn, or I'll blow your guts loose!"

Ed stepped back to the other side of the table, saying insistently: "The least you can do is to tell me what this man looks like. What you've said so far fits Bill Prall."

"His eyes are black, blacker than his hair," the girl said, that same mocking smile on her oval face that was even now beautiful. "And his name is David Fowler. I happen to know because he called at the office and introduced himself. He's from Philadelphia and new to this country. Does that satisfy you?"

Ed nodded, convinced now that the Eastern buyer was in reality Bill Prall, as he'd first suspected. He was remembering Prall's boast last night of being here on legitimate business. By shaving off beard and mustache, Prall's perpetually sallow face would give the impression that he was an Easterner as yet untanned by the strong sun. A city man's outfit, probably a black suit, white shirt, and string tie, would complete a convincing disguise.

Once again Ed was reminded that even though he was free, and not in this makeshift jail, Prall's word would count more than his and that no one would believe that Prall was the man really responsible for today's disappearance of Ledge's gold shipment.

"Is that all you have to ask me?" Nan queried, in biting words that cut in on his thoughts.

He nodded, somehow reluctant that she should be going even though each moment with her was an added torture to what he had already undergone today. It was painful to see

205

her standing there, proudly erect, beautiful, representing the thing he longed for more than anything in his life, yet as unattainable as the clearing of his name. He knew that he would always remember her as she was now, scornful of him, loathing him in every look and word. But this memory of her, coupled with last night's, he knew would be with him always.

Turning to the door, she said: "You'll have less than an hour to wait. Good bye, and I wish I'd never known you."

She was gone a moment later, and the complete darkness followed her as a symbol of the destruction once more of Ed's hopes. Minutes ago there had been a brief interval when that hope was renewed, but now it was gone, definitely, as surely as though it had never existed.

He took to pacing the floor, wondering whether or not he would take his chance when it came. This girl was giving him that chance only to ease her conscience, to know that she'd spared a man from death not out of love for him but out of pity, the same pity she had admitted she would give an animal, a snake. Looking back over the things she'd said, he forgot the passage of time. His thoughts went to Bill Prall, and he was as sure as he'd been before that Prall was the man serving up free drinks in the saloon.

The rôle Prall was playing was a subtle one. Sooner or later his whisky would prime the mob for a try at the jail. Ed had caught something in the stage office this morning that no one else had bothered to notice, the fact that Tom Hunter had counted more votes against his idea than for it. If the men gathered there were a fair representation of the town's feeling for him, it wouldn't take much of Prall's whisky to stir up the necessary anger for a lynching. Once that was accomplished, once Ed was finally out of the way, Prall would step in and with the very gold he had stolen buy up the claims out of which that gold had come. Many claim owners, disheartened over their impoverishment where they had expected riches, would want to get out of here, away from the futile task of grubbing a fortune from the earth. In the end, when the big Eastern mining interests did come in, Prall would be master, possessed of a wealth beyond his wildest dreams.

The rumble from the hillside above the street broke in on Ed's thoughts so suddenly that it startled him. When he had defined it, when he knew that the stacked logs at the sawmill were rolling down from their high shelf, he ran to the shack's back window and stared out into the darkness. The rumbling noise became a series of dull, low-toned explosions that he thought he recognized as massive logs bumping one against the other.

He could see nothing, but the sudden shout of the guard out there told him that his guess was correct. Shouts along the street took up the cry of the guard. All at once came the sound of splintering wood. Vaguely he saw the shape of a small lean-to being rolled in toward the shack's rear wall by what he saw was a huge pine log. He moved quickly away from the assay office's back wall, expecting each moment to hear the crash of wood on wood and see the wall belly inward.

There was a three second wait in which he felt the earth jarring beneath the floor. Then, from the saloon next door, came a rending crash and a series of shouts and cries. Hard on the heels of that first crash came others, yet the back wall of his room remained unbroken, solid. Finally, as quickly as it had come, the sound of splitting and rending wood faded out, and there was a momentary silence, broken almost immediately by the sound of men running along the plank walk outside.

Someone approached the guard out front, calling: "Get out back! I'll watch here! His gang rolled the logs down from the sawmill, trying to break him out. The back wall of the saloon's been busted in. We're damn' lucky it wasn't the shack."

Ed stepped to the back window. The eerie waving light of a lantern now lit up the littered yard in back of the saloon, where he had last night talked with Prall. The lean-to against which he and Prall had sat last night was a mass of wreckage of broken planks and torn sheets of tar paper that had once formed a roof. Ed saw then why Nan Hunter's plan had failed. The lean-to's wreckage had blocked the path of the rolling logs, had turned them aside so that, instead of coming directly on at the assay office, they had veered to crush in the saloon's back wall. The huge logs now lay piled in a disorderly upended stack across the yard in back of the saloon, a few uptilted and with butts pointing skyward. These, thrown out of a direct line by the lean-to's wreckage, had stopped the others.

As more men ran along the walk out front toward the saloon, they were warned clear of the assay office by the guard. Ed heard the man's voice calling insistently for the walks to be kept clear, and looked out the front window to see the crowd that was gathering in the street. There were defiant shouts and cries, while in the saloon next door the confusion had not yet died out. Lanterns appeared in the crowd on the street, and he could see men standing with clubs in their hands.

He realized soberly that Nan Hunter's plan

for his escape had only sealed the inevitability of the mob's breaking into the makeshift jail before morning, and of hanging the prisoner from a joist of the new store across the street. Even Tom Hunter wouldn't be able to talk the crowd into waiting.

Once more Ed started his pacing up and down the room. Now he carried in one hand a pair of long heavy tongs he had found near the furnace, expecting each moment to hear the grating of the lock on the door as the infuriated mob came in at him. The room was dimly lighted by the shifting glow of the lanterns from the street. His mind groped coolly for an idea that would show him a way out. For long minutes, as the shouts of the crowd blended to an angrily insistent roar out front, no idea came to him.

Each time as he walked the length of the small room, he was irritated at the way a certain board gave way under his boot and threw him off balance in mid-stride. Time and again this happened before he recognized exactly what it was. Once he understood it, he leaned down and pushed on the yielding board. Its end tilted downward an inch or two under the pressure of his hand.

In one split second the idea he had been searching for came to him in its entirety. Hardly had it taken shape in his mind before he was reaching back to press with one boot on the middle of the board, forcing its end above the level of the floor. His fingers went in under that end, and he pulled upward, slowly, with all his strength. The board creaked, the nails that held it grated against the pressure; then, suddenly, the whole length of the board came loose in his grasp.

He threw it aside and, using the stiff tongs as a lever, pried loose the adjoining board. It was more stubborn than the first, but in ten seconds he was lifting it clear of the floor, no longer careful now about the noise he made, for it was drowned out in the cries of the mob in the street.

He judged the width of the floor opening carefully before he stood erect and crossed the room to take down one of the ledgers off the back shelf. He opened it and tore out a handful of its sheets. All at once a thought stopped him, and he went to his knees and felt along the wall until his hands touched the folded square of tarpaulin. He opened it out and went to the front window, hanging the canvas over the window with its corners caught on the two upper edges of the frame. The glare of the lanterns from the street was immediately cut off, and the room plunged into total darkness.

Stepping to the back wall again, he wadded

the papers from the ledger and laid them at the base of the wall, in the corner made by the joining of a two-by-four joist and the wall's sheathing. He went to the shelf again and took down two more heavy ledgers, tearing them apart and adding their pages and torn covers to the pile of paper on the floor. Then, hurried by a sudden surge of shouts from the mob on the street, he took a match from his pocket and wiped it alight and touched it to the paper. It was slow in catching, but, once the flame was started, it mounted quickly up along the boards of the wall.

As the light of the flames from the heap of paper grew, he moved one of the chairs across to the door, wedging its back up under the door's knob. Last of all, he pushed the heavy center table against the chair. That done, he cast a final glance around the room and stepped down through the opening in the floor.

The floor joists of the building were set a bare two feet from the ground. Lying face up beneath the opening, he turned his head and could see faint lines of lantern light that shone through the planking of the wall ten feet out toward the street from him, for the shack's front wall ran along the back edge of the walk. The shouts of the crowd were amplified down here. He rolled over on his belly and crawled toward the walk, once looking back over his shoulder and out from beneath the shed and vaguely seeing the boots of the guard out back who stood near the rear wall. That sight, the knowledge that the guard could stoop down and see him and shoot him where he lay, made him move faster.

A winter's experience with snow and mud had taught the men of this boom camp that any building, or any structure, lying near the cañon bottom must be raised above the ground on firm foundations. The street being the very center of the cañon and at times running walk to walk with the rains that drained off the cañon slopes, the walks had been raised a foot, in places two feet, above the ground. Small boulders and piles of rock shards formed these foundations as well as those of the buildings flanking the walk.

Ed had remembered that, had gambled on the clearance of the plank walk from the ground when he let himself through the hole in the shack's floor. But now, as his hands went out before him in his crawl, his fingers touched the side of a walk joist and felt beneath it. There was only a bare six-inch space between joist and ground.

For a moment he lay there in utter helplessness, thinking that he had lost. Then, warned by a sudden lifting of shouts from the crowd, among them one voice that cried stridently — "Fire! The shack's afire!" — he rolled to one side and reached out again to feel the walk joist. This time the space beneath it was a good ten inches.

As the thud of boots sounded across the walk immediately over his head, he pushed head and shoulders in through that opening beneath the walk. Five seconds later he had edged to one side and his legs were in under the walk.

Above him, someone bellowed for an axe. Ed started crawling away from the assay office beneath the walk. Ten feet beyond where he had crawled under the walk, the ground sloped sharply downward, and there was almost enough clearance for him to crawl on hands and knees. He left the far corner of the assay office behind, crawled abreast the passageway next to the saloon. Then he was in front of the saloon, with the ground once more within bare inches of the walk overhead.

He had to stop there or dig his way on through and, reaching up ahead as far as he could feel, his fingers touched nothing but solid ground. Behind him the crowd had fallen strangely silent. A second later the sound of an axe striking wood rang out sharply, time and again. A sudden burst of shouts told him that the door to the assay office was down.

He was trapped here, more certainly than he'd been trapped in his jail. It would take only seconds for the men in the office to beat out the fire and discover what had happened to him.

Then, miraculously, came a shout from the office: "Get some buckets! Hell, we can't see for the smoke!" Looking out from under the walk's edge, Ed caught the reflected rosy light of flames, and sight of that put hope in him once more. He edged backward, knowing that the fire would have to be put out before the mob could enter the building and find out what had happened to him.

Four feet back from the hump of earth that had stopped him, he crawled in toward the saloon's front wall. The boards of the wall ran clear to the ground around the building. But Ed worked his long body at right angles to that boarded-up foundation and kicked hard with his boots. At the second try a board buckled. He pushed it inward and crawled through the opening, in under the saloon.

It was while he was working his way toward the saloon's rear that a wild shout from the crowd told him that the fire was out and that his escape had been discovered. He crawled faster, blindly, hitting his head on the floor joists, crawling around hummocks of ground that blocked his way. Finally his reaching hands felt an obstruction he couldn't understand. It was round, and along its length he felt rough wood bark.

Suddenly he knew what it was, one of the logs that had been rolled down from the sawmill. He moved to one side and followed the log along its length. Within six feet he came to the point where it had broken through the boards of the foundation. The jagged-edged opening was big enough for him to worm through.

As he came to his feet in the yard back of the saloon, a man ran around the near corner within ten feet of him. Ed lunged and struck out wildly, his fist catching the man on the shoulder and throwing him back off his feet. Ed wheeled and ran the other way, jumping into the maze of logs that cluttered the yard. Behind him someone shouted, and a gun's explosion beat the air. The air rush of the bullet fanned his cheek as he threw himself down behind a wall of logs and crawled on hands and knees toward the back of the yard.

He moved quickly to one side, came erect again, and in three strides was rounding the corner of a shed behind the harness shop that adjoined the saloon. Two more shots beat the air, and at the corner of the shed's wall a wood splinter flew out from a board, gashing his cheek. Then he had the shed between him and the saloon and was headed up the cañon's steep side slope at a run. Twenty yards farther on he had the spreading branches of a tall cedar for protection. More guns took up the staccato thunder of the first, but the firing back there was wild, aimed blindly to cover the slope up which he ran.

He didn't stop until he had climbed half-way to the cañon's rim, and only then because his lungs could no longer drag in enough air to give him the strength to climb farther. He kept down the panic brought on at seeing the glow of lanterns below coming nearer, knowing that he could pit his own endurance against any man's in camp. When he moved on again, he worked on a line parallel with the cañon bottom, no longer climbing but heading up the cañon and toward the peaks. It was natural that they would think he was headed out, down the cañon.

Half an hour later he had put the winking lights of Ledge out of sight behind him and was covering the gently sloping ground through the timber that lay above the diggings. He had a few bad moments when he came abruptly on a slab shack squatting on a high shelf among the trees. He was about to retrace his steps when a thought took him on.

He approached the shack soundlessly and stood a mere foot short of its low door and listened for five long minutes. No sound came from inside. He reached out and tugged at the rawhide latch string of the door. The latch bar raised and let the door swing inward on squeaking hinges. Once more he drew back and waited, expecting the sound of the owner stirring inside. It didn't come. At length, he took two quick soundless steps that carried him in through the open door. Still no sound. After a long half minute's wait, he lit a match. The room, the bunk at its far end, was empty.

When Ed left the cabin three minutes later, he was carrying a rifle and a .45 Colt sagged from a scarred holster at his thigh. One of his trouser pockets bulged with shells for the Winchester and each loop of the gun's belt held a fresh load.

Instead of keeping on up the cañon, he worked down to the faint line of a trail and started back toward Ledge. He was remembering one thing only, that Bill Prall's men couldn't have headed out this morning after getting the gold, for there was no way for them to have passed the stage without being seen. It naturally followed that Prall's hide-out, if he had one, lay up the cañon and that his men were there. And Ed, wanting to discover where that hide-out lay, was taking the most direct means that occurred to him of doing that very thing.

Sooner or later, tonight perhaps, Prall would want to send word up to his men of what had happened in town and how they were to get out of the cañon and dispose of the gold. He had bragged that his men, with the exception of Ben Frost, didn't know who they were working for. So it would be Ben Frost who would sometime tonight or early tomorrow head for the hide-out.

Ed retraced his steps as far as the upper limits of the street, within sight of the town's last shack. There he squatted in the deep shadow of a rock outcropping and, Winchester cradled across his knees, built a smoke and lit it. That cigarette was the first of many he smoked on his long watch.

CHAPTER SIX

Bill Prall caught Ben Frost's eye on his way out of the saloon less than half an hour after Ed had made the break from the assayer's office. By a brief nod of the head Prall signaled Frost that he should follow him. Out on the street, he paused long enough to take a cigar from the tooled leather case he carried in the inside pocket of his fine broadcloth coat. Lighting the cigar, he glanced back over his shoulder and saw that Ben was coming out the swing doors. He sauntered unhurriedly down the walk and turned in at the hotel and walked down its long uncarpeted hallway to the room at the rear.

He had taken off his coat and loosened his starched collar when the room's door opened. Ben Frost came in, took a last look down the hallway, and softly closed the door. He turned around, a worried frown on his face, and said in a low voice: "This is a hell of a note."

"Not so bad." Prall sat on the bed, hooked a boot in the rung of a chair by the wall, and pulled it closer to him, indicating that Frost should take it. When Ben was seated, Prall said: "How's everything at the camp?"

"It'd be better if I could give 'em something to do. They've got the itch to get out and spend some of that dust they split this afternoon. What's next, boss?"

"Ed Thorn."

A wry smile twisted Ben Frost's ugly face. "You aren't havin' much luck with Thorn, are you?"

"Want to lay a bet that I can't have my hands on him by sunup tomorrow?"

Frost shook his head, his glance growing more respectful. "You never bet unless it's a sure thing. But how're you goin' to swing it?"

Instead of answering directly, Prall said: "If you were Ed Thorn and knew what he knows, would you high-tail or stick around here and try and clear your name?"

"I'd stick, providin' I had his mulish guts."

Prall nodded. "Which is exactly what he'll do. He knows we've got a crew workin' for us. The first thing he'll do will be to try and locate the camp."

Frost's face settled into a belligerent look. "I'll warn the boys."

"Better than that, you'll toll Thorn straight to the camp."

Ben's look was one of slow-gathering incredulity. "Why? That's invitin' sure trouble."

"It isn't if you'll send a couple men out into the brush directly after you get there. They can swing downcañon a ways and wait until Thorn walks up to the fire and throws down on the rest of you. When he does, they can take him from behind."

Frost's expression eased into a wide grin. "When's all this goin' to happen?"

"Now. Tonight. The moon's bright. It'll make the job easy for Thorn to follow you."

"What do I do with him, when I have him?"

"Tie him up and leave him at the camp. Then come back here. You've been seen in town and no one's wise to why you're here. When you. . . ."

"Hold on! You're forgettin' the old jasper that drives the stage. He knows damn' well who I am. I've had a hell of a time dodgin' him."

"He's gone now. Drove a stageload of men down the cañon this afternoon. They've put guards across the cañon to keep our bunch from breakin' out. I heard tonight that this Belden, the driver, has gone on to Plainsville to see the sheriff and have him send out for some bloodhounds to run down our bunch." A smug smile came to Prall's face. "It'll take three days for the bloodhounds to get here. By that time it won't matter."

"But what about this driver? By the time I've tolled Thorn into camp and come back here, he may be here to give me away."

"Not if you start now. Belden can't possibly get back before three or four in the mornin'. He's got a bum arm, and he'll be takin' it easy."

"All right," Ben agreed reluctantly. "What do I do after I get back from camp?"

"Come to the hotel here and wake up Tom Hunter. Tell him you've been in town only a few days and that you've prospected up the cañon a bit. Today, while you were lookin' for color a few miles above town, you ran into a camp with half a dozen men in it. You didn't think much about it until tonight, when you came down and heard the story of a gang stealin' the gold. You still don't know that the men in that camp aren't prospectors, like you. But you thought you'd mention it to him."

Ben Frost's flaccid face took on a slow smile. "Givin' the bunch the double-cross?" he asked.

"Why not?" Prall shrugged. "Hunter'll know what to do. He'll get up a posse and go up there to take a look at that camp, with you as guide. I'll try to come along, too. When we get to the camp, we open up. Thorn will be cut down with the rest. It'll tie him in with the

223

bunch. He'll die either then or at the end of a rope later."

"Supposin' he talks?"

Prall laughed soundlessly. "Supposin' he does? Who's goin' to believe him? I've got papers provin' I'm Dave Fowler from Philadelphia."

Tilting back in his chair, Frost sat a moment considering. At length he said: "What about their share of the gold?"

"You know where it is. We'll wait'll things calm down, then go up there and split it."

"How?"

"A third for you, two-thirds for me."

Frost's chair came down on all four legs with a thud. "Half and half."

Prall shook his head. "Unh-uh, Ben."

Ben Frost's face purpled darkly. Then some inner thought tempered his belligerence with caution as he said complainingly: "You can push a man too far, Bill."

"Not you," Prall said suavely. "Remember that reward out for you in Arizona."

That threat wiped out the last trace of active rebellion in Ben Frost. He stood up, said in a surly voice: "You want me to start now?"

Prall nodded, and watched his man go out the door. Long after Ben Frost had gone, a shadowy smug smile held on Prall's long, cadaverous face.

CHAPTER SEVEN

The past hour had been a bad one for Ed Thorn, with the moon's half disc hanging above the line of the peaks to remind him of last night's walk up the cañon with Nan Hunter. Because any thought of the girl represented his blasted hopes, he was thankful for the interruption made by a man leaving the end of the street and walking noisily toward him upcañon, taking no care to conceal his approach.

In the ghostly, deceiving light of the moon, Ed at first thought that this nocturnal walker might be one of the claim workers from the diggings above, returning to his camp after the night's excitement. But when the man was almost abreast of him, he suddenly recognized Ben Frost's burly shape, and a flood of excitement went through him. He let Frost get almost forty yards ahead before he edged out from behind the outcropping, Winchester cradled in the crook of his elbow, and followed.

More than once in the next half hour, as he climbed up the cañon, soundlessly following Prall's man, he wondered at Ben's carelessness in keeping to the open and not once looking back. Then he thought he had the answer to it. Ben knew that every man in the diggings was in town tonight and that the cañon was as deserted as the shack Ed had raided earlier. That explained, Ed was thankful that circumstances made following Ben as easy as though he'd done it in the broad light of day.

Higher up, a full three miles above Ledge, the cañon narrowed abruptly, its width choked with stately cedars and aspen and, here and there, a tangle of scrub-oak thickets. Frost walked through the brush with no pretense at going silently, making Ed's job of shouldering through the thickets much easier than it would have been had he followed a more watchful quarry. Rock ledges and abrupt turnings made the going hard at times, but in these places Frost would pause to get his wind, not once looking behind him. Once, when he stood for five minutes making and smoking a cigarette, Ed stood close enough to him to catch the pale cloud of tobacco smoke each time he exhaled.

Ed came on the fire around a turning so abruptly that, when he first saw its ruddy glow, barely twenty yards separated him from it. He heard distinctly the flat challenge of a guard and Ben Frost's grumbled answer. Standing where he was, Ed saw the vague shadows of men rise up from their blankets and move beyond the dying red coals of the fire. He heard a muttered undertone of talk, and a full minute later Ben Frost threw an armload of dry cedar on the coals. In a few moments they had caught and blazed up, broadening the circle of light until Ed found himself standing almost within it.

He acted on impulse then, thinking that somehow he could disarm those men and take them back down the cañon as visible proof to Tom Hunter of his innocence. He thumbed back the hammer of the Winchester and, holding it ready, stepped in toward the fire.

When he was within fifteen feet of Ben Frost's turned back, he stopped, planted his boots wide apart, and drawled: "Reach, Ben!"

Frost wheeled around in surprise. The three men across the fire from him stiffened. Then Ben saw the leveled Winchester and called crisply: "Don't fool with him, gents! It's Thorn!"

Ben's hands came up, as did those of his men behind him.

Ed said tonelessly: "Shuck out your irons
. . . slow."

Ben Frost's hands moved down to his guns.
He deliberately lifted them clear of leather
and then let them drop to the ground alongside, his men following suit. Then, strangely,
a tight smile came to Ben's face and he was
saying: "Look behind you, Ed."

Ed didn't move, fearing a trap. Ben understood his wariness and his smile broadened.
He called — "Sing out, Slade!" — and a moment later Ed heard the snap of a branch behind him.

A voice close at hand, immediately behind,
said flatly: "I ain't never shot a man in the
back before. Don't make me now, Thorn."

Turning to face that voice, Ed was careful
to lower the muzzle of the rifle. Behind him
stood two men, each with a pair of guns lined
at him. He understood in an instant the reason for Ben's seeming carelessness on his
walk up here, understood that he had been
nicely tricked and that Bill Prall's brain lay
behind this simple ruse.

Ben said: "Better unload your hardware,
Ed." His tone was mocking, yet it was one
that couldn't be contradicted.

Ed dropped the Winchester's butt to the
ground, let go the barrel, and unbuckled the
shell belt about his waist. His weapons on the

ground, he turned and sauntered over to the fire.

Ben Frost stepped back out of his reach, then said sharply to one of his men: "Slade, you're good at knots. Tie him up."

One of the pair who had come up behind Ed, a spare-framed youth with a mask of premature wickedness stamped on his fair cheeks, came across to the fire and caught a coil of rope tossed over to him. In five minutes Slade had laced Ed as securely with the rope as a straight-jacket could have held him. It was a job expertly done by Slade's sure fingers, the windings not too tight to stop circulation but too firm to give the least fraction of an inch.

Ben Frost witnessed this with a smug smile etched on his loose face. At length, when Slade came to his feet and observed his handiwork, Ben said: "I gave you credit for havin' more sense than this, Ed. Prall didn't. He was right, as usual." He turned to face his men. "You can hit your blankets again. I'm headed back to town to see the boss. Be back early in the mornin'."

He took a last look at Ed, and then walked out of the circle of the firelight. Two minutes later the sound of his going downcañon had died out in the night air.

Ed saw that young Slade was looking at

him. A thin, mirthless smile was on Slade's face. He spoke back over his shoulder to the men beyond the fire. "We'll toss to see who stays up with him."

They gathered around the blaze, and a coin was tossed. Slade cursed softly and came back to Ed's side of the fire as the others took to their blankets. He squatted on his heels near Ed and took out tobacco and built a smoke.

Presently Ed said, loud enough so that they all could hear: "You're a sucker, Slade."

The youth's glance came slowly around to him. "You want me to stuff some rags in your mouth?" he said with no show of emotion.

"Better hear what I have to say first."

Slade tossed his cigarette into the fire, came to his feet, and started unknotting the bandanna from his throat, his purpose plainly to carry out his threat of gagging Ed.

One of the men beyond the blaze called: "Let's hear what he has to say, Slade. Hell, I ain't had a good laugh for a month."

Slade paused, shrugged finally, and squatted on his heels once more.

Ed shifted a little to ease the strain of the ropes on his arms. He lay on his back, looking up at the star-studded dome of the heavens, and, as he spoke, he was trying to imagine the looks on the faces of Prall's men. "You're all pretty smart or you wouldn't have been picked for this job," he began. "But the man you're working for, Bill Prall, stays a jump ahead of any man he hires. He's two jumps ahead of the bunch of you right now."

He paused, and in the drawn-out silence that followed his words not a sound came from his listeners. Finally Slade said in a mocking, high falsetto voice: "Tell us some more about the big bad man, gran'ma!"

A laugh or two came from the men across the fire. Ed ignored them, went on: "I know Prall, know him like a book. I've been thinkin' what I'd do in his place. First of all, he'd give his right arm to make me eat crow, and he will before he's through. The best way I know for him to do that is to turn me in as one of the gang that took that gold this morning. When he makes a sucker out of me, he makes suckers out of you."

Across there, a man stirred in his blankets. Ed turned his head and saw that the man was sitting up, looking at him with an ugly questioning glance. "Say that again," the man drawled.

"This Ben Frost is Prall's understrapper," Ed said. "Between them, they'll use you until they're through with you, which is about now. Wouldn't it make Prall kingpin of this camp if he could take the whole lot of us, me included, and get rid of us in a bunch?"

"Let him try it," came the man's flat statement.

"He will."

Ed let that two-word assertion lie without elaboration. Ten seconds of utter silence without any man protesting told him that it had hit the mark. These men were innately suspicious, as was only natural in men engaged in the business they were.

Finally, when the pause had been long enough, he said: "Ben Frost knows where you've hid your share of the gold, doesn't he?"

The man across the fire said curtly: "I told you we shouldn't have let Frost. . . ."

"Yates!" Slade snapped, to cut in on the other's words. "You're spooky as an old woman . . . have been ever since the first day you bought in on this deal. The whole damned lot of you turn in and get some sleep. This jasper's tryin' to talk his way out of a tight spot, and you're takin' the bait like a bunch of hungry minnows."

Yates said in a surly tone: "What he's sayin' makes sense to me."

Ed put in: "How about the rest of you? Are you with Yates or Slade?"

Before anyone had the time to answer his query, Slade took two quick steps that put him alongside Ed. He drew back a booted foot and kicked Ed savagely, hard, in the side. Ed's breath soughed out of his lungs in a convulsive gasp, and, as he choked back a cry of pain and tried to drag breath back into his empty lungs, Slade looked down at him with a malevolent smile imprinted on his face. He said: "Keep that underslung lip of yours buttoned, big wind, or, by God, I'll mash your teeth down your throat!"

Across the fire, Yates said tonelessly: "You'll answer for that, Slade."

Slade turned on him, arms cocked, fingers clawed over the handles of his guns: "Want to try and make me now, Yates?"

Another voice said mildly: "Yates, you're loco as hell! Sleep it off. Tomorrow mornin's time enough to talk this over."

Slade seemed to relax. He resumed his former place beside the fire and hunkered down on his heels once more. Yates, with a last glowering look at the young gunman, lay back in his blankets. Stillness settled down over the camp, a stillness at first broken only by the faint night sounds and finally by the deep breathing and the snores of the men in their blankets around the fire.

Ed lay wide awake, and his mind was running back over what he had accomplished by his suggestion that Ben Frost might double-cross his men. He himself didn't believe in

Ben's treachery at first, but, as he thought more about it, about Prall's part in the gold robbery, betrayal of the gang seemed the logical thing to follow. Yet, finally believing that, he was powerless to do anything about it. He could only hope that for once Bill Prall's keen mind wouldn't see the chance offered, the chance of silencing every man who had worked for him, the chance of getting rid of Ed Thorn, who knew more against him than any man alive besides Ben Frost, and Prall had said that Frost would never talk, would never dare to.

The minutes dragged on into hours, the fire's coals dying down until Ed, only ten feet out, lay in total darkness. He set about furtively testing the ropes that bound him and, after ten long minutes of trying each strand within the reach of his hand, had to admit that they would have held him for days, maybe weeks, without loosening. Slade had done a workman-like job. If he was going to get free, it would have to be by a way other than fighting his way out of these ropes.

He had no knowledge of the passage of time, his mind being so full of the quick reversal of luck since last night's talk with Nan Hunter. A lot had happened today, too much for him to take in except by careful consideration. But when all the elements lay clearly in his mind, he was sobered by the awful ring of circumstances that had dragged him down. At some point his plans of betraying Prall today had gone astray. Or had Prall from the first known how he would act in giving his plan away?

In the end the answer lay as obscurely as in the beginning, with Bill Prall assuming an almost superhuman quality of insight. The man was shrewd, cunning, as cunning in this play as he'd been in concealing his part in the Montana stage hold-up. That, added to today's misfortune, seemed an overwhelming indictment against Ed's name, one he'd never live to see lifted . . . if he, indeed, could hope of living even a day longer. Whatever was to happen to him would happen swiftly now. Bill Prall would force his hand, now that things were again running his way.

He was thinking of these things, trying to make order of the turmoil of thoughts that ranged his fevered mind, when suddenly a shape loomed above him, Slade's shape, and a hand was clamped over his mouth. Then Slade was bending down so that his mouth was close to Ed's ear, whispering: "Don't make a sound, Thorn. I'm with you on this, the same as Yates thought he was. Listen to me and you'll be out of here in short order."

Ed nodded, and Slade's hand eased off his

mouth. Slade went on in that low, barely audible whisper: "Here's the way I've figured it. Frost is forked, as forked as a rattler's tongue. In his place, I'd turn in the whole bunch, only I wouldn't wait. If it's to be done at all, he'll do it tonight. And when he comes up here, you and me aren't goin' to be within shootin' distance."

Ed whispered: "Now you're usin' your head, Slade."

The gunman ignored this, continuing: "I'm goin' out of here with the gold. You're goin' with me because I can't swing it alone. But you'll go without a gun, and your first break will net you a bullet in your spine. Understand?"

Once again Ed nodded.

"Here's the lay, then. The horses are in a corral above, far enough so we can snake 'em out without wakin' the others. The gold's a dozen rods above the corral. Fred Bates is standin' guard on it. We'll get rid of him, load the gold on a jughead, and head up the cañon. I've done some strayin' around in the week we've been here. They claim there's no way out of the head of the cañon. I know different. Are you with me?"

"For a share of the gold," Ed said, sensing that he must play a greedy part if he was to deceive Slade.

"We'll split it two ways," Slade agreed too readily. "But until we're clear, I'm the boss. Once we're over the hills, we split, and you've got my word on it. Now roll over so I can use this knife."

Ed rolled onto his side, and a second later felt the cool touch of steel at his wrists. Shortly, the tension of the rope eased away from his lower arms. In ten more seconds he was sitting upright, his arms free, and Slade was working at the bonds around his legs.

Slade helped pull him to his feet, and for the five seconds they stood there, waiting for the numbness to leave Ed's legs, the gunman's eyes shuttled nervously over the sleeping figures beyond the fire. Finally Ed signaled that he could walk, and Slade nodded up the cañon. Ed understood clearly that he was to lead the way, that from now on Slade's guns would be at his back, threatening him, that he would live only so long as Slade had use for him. After that, once Slade thought he was safe, he would dispose of Ed quickly and expertly, taking the gold and heading out with it for a new country.

Keyed to a wariness he knew was necessary if they were going to clear the camp without waking the others, Ed moved soundlessly around the fire, beyond it, and into the brush above. Slade moved so silently behind him that once he turned to make sure the man was there. Slade was only two steps behind him, moving with a cat-like grace that matched his own. Fifty yards above camp Slade said quietly: "Swing off to the left, near the wall. The corral's up yonder."

They came to the corral, a crude one built of unpeeled aspen poles, five minutes later. Ed went to the gate, let down the top bar, and Slade said from behind him: "Wait here. I'd better take care of Bates first thing."

His spare outline faded into the thick shadows, and Ed noticed for the first time that the moon had dipped beyond the peaks, that now only the faint starlight relieved the night's obscure blackness. He leaned back against the corral gate, wondering if his chances would be better in running now and not going with Slade. Yet an ingrained sense of caution, coupled with the knowledge that Slade might be waiting out there in the darkness, gun ready and expecting just such a move, compelled him to stay where he was.

It took a strong force of will to put down his nervousness as he made his choice to go on with Slade. Finding the gold was of first importance. Once that was safely within his sight, he could watch his chances to get away from Slade. An insistent worry built up in him, backed by the knowledge that even in possession of a large share of the gold he still lacked proof against Bill Prall, but he bridled this worry with the fatalistic outlook of taking each thing in its turn. When Slade came up out of the shadows a few minutes afterward, he was once more master of himself, as nerveless as when holding the ribbons of a lurching stage. He had his chance, and he'd make it count.

Time passed swiftly then as they climbed into the corral and cut out three horses from the dozen in the string. Slade took him a few yards out from the corral to where half a dozen saddles were thrown over a pole beneath the wide-spreading branches of a tall cedar. They found a pack saddle, too, and made short work of saddling their own mounts along with a lead horse.

When that was finished and they were ready to go, Slade once again cautioned Ed to go first: "We'll walk," he said. "Follow your nose. You'll likely trip over Bates."

It happened almost that way. Twenty rods above the corrals, in the thick brush that choked the entire width of the cañon bottom Ed saw now an outstretched figure on the ground in a small clearing immediately in front of him barely in time to keep from stumbling over it. He didn't stoop down to examine Bates, but the inhuman angle at which the man's head sloped away from his shoulders told him that Slade had broken his neck. Beyond the body, a darker shadow of mounded earth told Ed that Slade had dug up the gold. Two strides farther on showed him the small stack of burlap bags.

For the second time that day, Ed handled those heavy sacks, each bulging with twenty or thirty small rawhide pokes that marked the shares of individual claim owners. Back at the corral, Slade had found a torn and rotten piece of heavy canvas. He now rigged this into a makeshift sling between the crossed arms of the pack saddle and loaded the gold sacks into it. A rope finally held the bundle securely to the cross arms, and they were ready to travel.

"You'll lead," Slade said curtly. "There isn't a trail beyond here, so get there the best way you know how." He slapped the holster along his right thigh with an open palm. "And remember, Thorn."

He let that last word carry flatly, menacingly, before he nodded and swung into the saddle of his bay pony. Ed, taking the lead rope of the gray packing the gold, climbed lithely into the hull and immediately started on up the cañon.

From time to time, Slade's voice would sound out behind, calling — "Left." or "Right." or "Better swing into those trees." —

as they went on. It was slow work, the cañon's narrow limits and swiftly climbing brush-choked slopes making the going hard.

They had been at it twenty minutes and, as Ed judged, covered less than two miles, when suddenly from downcañon racketed up the explosions of guns muffled by distance. Ed instinctively drew rein and turned in the saddle at the sound. Dimly, behind him, he could see Slade's outline. Slade was faced around, too.

Slade said — "There's the wind-up." — and brought his head around again, touching his spurs to his pony's flanks to go on. But the bay wouldn't move on, standing as he was with muzzle to the rump of the pack horse.

A sudden flood of warning cocked Slade's body rigid. Ed's pony stood immediately before the pack horse. The saddle was empty.

Slade's right hand blurred to his thigh and lifted clear the short-barreled .45. He caught a whisper of sound close out from his left stirrup and instinctively rolled away from that side of his horse, swinging up his gun. Then Ed's springing shape lunged up out of the darkness of the ground close alongside, moving too fast for Slade's hand to come around.

The gunman, his gun in his speeding and deft hand, let out a choked cry of fear as Ed's fist arced up at him. The slamming of Ed's fist on the point of his shelving jaw cut off that cry in a smothered gasp. Slade's right arm stopped its frantic upward swing, his head tilted crazily back, and all at once he was falling loosely, in the way of a man struck down by sudden unconsciousness.

Ed stepped around the rearing pony and caught Slade's falling, inert form in his arms. He ground-haltered the bay and dragged Slade a few feet to one side. Then, quickly, he unbuckled the gunman's twin belts and cinched them about his own waist, thonging holsters low on thighs. He inspected each gun, rocking open the loading gates and spinning the cylinders to make sure the loads were fresh. As he dropped the guns into leather once more, a renewed burst of firing came from downcañon, the explosions ripping upward along the corridor between the high walls in sharp, staccato sounds.

He walked up to his own horse and took the rope from the horn of the saddle. Lifting Slade's slight body, he threw it belly down across the saddle and tied his wrists and boots beneath the pony's belly. Ten turns of rope about the cinch bound Slade securely. With a last, inspecting glance that satisfied him, Ed cut the pony's reins, rigged a length of rope from the bridle to the pack saddle on the horse ahead, and went up to slope into his own saddle.

He reined around and started back down the cañon, using his spurs whenever he came to the scant open stretches. The sound of the guns down there was stilled now. The settling silence that held the night air became ominous, threatening. Yet there was no question of what to do in Ed's mind. He kept straight on, trusting to the hunch that was guiding him.

CHAPTER EIGHT

Tom Hunter planned it all well, taking three quarters of an hour in leading his twelve men the last two hundred yards up the brush-choked limits of the cañon and placing them about the camp. He had at least ten men he knew he could count on, two others he didn't know much about — the stranger who had brought the news of the camp to town an hour ago and the city man in the fine broad-cloth suit who had given out so much free whisky at the saloon tonight before the jail-break. He hadn't wanted to bring the city man, who claimed to be a buyer for a big Eastern mining outfit, but in the end the man's insistence, coupled with his impatience, prevailed, and Hunter hadn't waited to argue.

Now, looking down from the ledge where he lay and seeing the dying red coals of the fire centering the small clearing directly below, Tom Hunter's glance counted four blanket-covered figures on the upcañon side of the fire. He looked at his watch, judging that he'd given his men enough time to get their places and aim their guns. The camp was surrounded.

He elbowed up on the ledge and, kneeling, cupped his hands to his mouth and let out the deep-toned shout that was the prearranged signal. One of the shapes below in the blankets stirred, sat up. Hunter had given the order that no one was to fire into the camp unless someone down there either made a break for it or used a gun. Things were going nicely as Hunter shouted a second time: "Throw up your hands. Wake your partners and tell 'em we've got a dozen. . . ."

Crack!

A rifle's sharp explosion cut in on his words. The man down there gave a convulsive jerk, staggered uncertainly to his feet, his hands clawing his chest.

Crack!

A second rifle, directly across from Hunter, exploded to punctuate the exact instant the wounded man doubled up and jackknifed prone on his face. The three other blanket-shrouded figures down there moved, two of them coming erect.

Hunter shouted: "Damn you, hold your fire!"

Hardly had he spoken when another rifle

laid a clap of sharp thunder into the cañon's narrow corridor. One of the men in the camp screamed wildly and started at a crippled run for the brush along the wall immediately below Hunter. The two others, seeing one of their number shot down in cold blood, also broke and ran.

Tom Hunter cursed savagely time and again as other guns took up the firing of the first pair. He had wanted to take those men alive. But now, in the quick burst of shots that racketed up along the cañon, his hopes were blasted in a scant two seconds. He knelt there on the ledge, horror-stricken, and watched the three remaining men of the camp cut down as cold-bloodedly as steers in a slaughterhouse.

It was over in less than thirty seconds, or nearly over. A brief moment after the rifles of his posse had become silent, one fallen man who lay close in to the margins of a thicket surged suddenly to his feet and lunged for shelter. Two rifles threw their lead at him, the same two rifles that had opened the firing in the beginning. The man stumbled, got to his feet again, and reached the brush. He was nearly hidden by it when he threw up his hands and, body broken sickeningly backward as a lead slug broke his spine, fell out into the clearing with a choked, hoarse cry of death blending with the echoes of the rifles that had cut him down.

Shortly, the men of the posse straggled out of the brush ringing the camp. They made a hurried inspection of the four bodies, and then gathered silently in the clearing. Hunter, wild with anger, climbed down off the ledge and joined them. Someone found a few sticks of dry wood and threw them on the coals. The sticks caught and blazed up, giving an eerie, uncertain light.

No one spoke for a full minute. Only two of the posse dared to meet Tom Hunter's beetling glance. Finally one of them said: "Don't look at me that way, Tom. Hell, I ain't burned an ounce of powder tonight."

"Who did it?" Hunter asked in low and deadly tones. His glance swung around the half circle of faces.

For a long moment, a stolid silence met his question. At length, the man in the broadcloth suit, the Eastern buyer, spoke up: "I take it I'm to blame, sir. But when that first man got up out of his blankets, I saw he had two guns in his hands. If you don't believe it, go over there and take a look. I thought he'd spotted one of our men and was about to shoot him."

A posseman moved away from the fire, striding over to where the blankets lay. In a moment, he called: "He's right, Hunter. Here's his guns. I reckon this stranger saw better than the rest of us."

"But why the hell did you have to shoot him?" Hunter blazed impotently. He realized that his men had taken seriously the words of the mining man, that, enraged over the loss of their gold, what had happened seemed a logical act of vengeance. Helplessly his glance went to the stranger who had tonight brought in the news of the men camped up here. "You!" he said. "You were across there and opened up after he did." He jerked a thumb to indicate the mining man. "I want to know why the hell you didn't use your head and let me call down that we had the camp surrounded?"

The stranger's loose face took on a sullen scowl. "How was I to know who had started the shootin'? You said, if they made a break for it, to open up. I thought it was you that threw that first shot."

"Me, too, Tom," put in another to convince Tom Hunter of the futility of further argument.

Hunter shrugged his wide shoulders, letting out a gusty oath of anger. "Well, there's nothing to do about it now. Dead men can't very well talk. A hell of a chance we got now of finding out where the gold is. Pack 'em back down the cañon to town."

"We could have a look around first," someone said, and immediately it was agreed that the camp and its surroundings should be searched. Two men went below to get the lanterns that had been left with the man stationed with the horses. For twenty minutes the lanterns' waving lights moved around the camp. Two men came back with the word that a corral had been found above and, above that, a man lying dead with a broken neck beside a scooped-out hole in the earth.

Had Tom Hunter been watching the mining man and the stranger who had brought them up here, he would have seen a swift interchange of glances and a cold frown settle across the long and narrow face of the mining man. But Hunter was disgusted with what had happened tonight, sickened by the sight of the wholesale killing, and said abruptly: "The rest can wait until morning. We're going back."

The four bodies were carried down to the horses, packed across saddles, and the posse made its way back to town, four of the ponies carrying double. Ledge's street was strangely lighted and busy for this early morning hour before dawn. Hunter and his posse had left town quietly. But the sound of the guns had roused a few light sleepers, and the word had

249

spread. The walks were alive with restlessly moving groups, and a crowd had formed, as usual, in front of the saloon. The posse turned in at the tie rack there, and the bodies were carried in and laid on three poker tables, shoved together and draped with canvas to save the green felt from being stained by blood.

Dan Belden was in the crowd of curious onlookers who met the posse out front and soberly watched the laying out of the four dead men. Dan caught the look on Tom Hunter's face and stayed away from the stage owner, knowing his temper and deciding that morning would be soon enough to get the story of what happened while he'd been on the way back from Plainsville. He saw Nan Hunter on the hotel's narrow verandah and went up there to stand with her, watching the traffic come and go from the saloon.

"Dan," the girl asked quietly, two minutes after he had come to stand beside her. "Was . . . did you see the bodies?"

He understood her question and looked down at her, smiling gently and saying: "He wasn't one of 'em, Nan."

She gave him a look of thankfulness, and he caught the keen relief in her eyes. Then he looked back toward the saloon again, idly eyeing a few of the possemen who had gathered at the hitch rail and were answering the questions of the crowd. The mining man, Fowler, came up the steps, wished them a polite — "Good night." — and went down the hallway to his room.

All at once Dan saw a man whose thick shape was familiar to him, there in the group along the saloon's walk. In another instant he'd recognized Ben Frost. Sight of Frost, whom he knew to be one of the gang that had stolen the gold, made Dan excuse himself from the girl and go quickly across to the stage station. He unlocked the door and went inside to get a gun down from the shelf over his cot. He rammed the gun through the waistband of his trousers and came back out onto the walk, locking the door behind him.

Then, sauntering idly across the street, he approached the group of possemen at the tie rail. For a minute he listened to their talk, then moved on unobtrusively in between two of the haltered horses until he stood immediately behind Ben Frost.

He lifted the gun from his belt and reached out with it, ramming its snout into the gunman's spine, saying crisply: "Frost, there's a slug here for you, if you draw too deep a breath."

His tones cut clearly above the other voices. Those nearby turned to face him. He went on: "Someone get Tom Hunter. Here's the man the wild bunch busted out of jail down in Plainsville last week!"

The men alongside Ben Frost at the tie rail turned and backed away. Those near the door of the saloon, directly in line with Dan's gun, hurried to move out of line.

Someone in the saloon called — "Hunter, you're wanted out here!" — and a moment later Tom Hunter's high frame moved out through the doors.

"Tom, I've got you a man to work on," Dan Belden drawled. "He's the jasper Thorn and me turned over to the sheriff last week, the one that held up the stage."

Hunter's square face went blank. He eyed Ben Frost, who stood, stiff and unmoving, under the threat of Dan's gun. Dan reached out and unbuckled Frost's belts. They fell to the plank walk with a loud thud that punctuated the momentary silence.

Hunter said curtly — "Bring him in here!" — and willing hands gripped Ben Frost's arms and pushed him roughly on across the walk and in through the swing doors.

So strained was the attention of the crowd, that no one had seen the rider who came down the street, holding the lead rope of two ponies, and turned in at the hitch rail in front of the assayer's office. Dan Belden was ducking beneath the tie rail, about to follow the men who were leading Ben Frost into the saloon, when Ed Thorn's voice called clearly: "Dan!"

CHAPTER NINE

Dan Belden stopped short at the sound of that voice and turned slowly to face it, recognizing it instantly. In the light from a side window of the saloon he saw Ed Thorn sitting stiffly in the saddle, a pair of guns in his hands. Those guns moved in slow arcs that covered the men nearest along the walk.

"Dan, come over here!" Ed called.

Someone at the inside edge of the walk recognized Ed's voice and took a step toward the swing doors. The gun in Ed's right hand exploded to lay flat echoes along the street. A splinter of wood flew from the door frame a bare two inches above the man's head, and Ed drawled: "Everyone stay planted! Dan, come across here!"

Those inside the saloon crowded toward the doors on the heel of the shot and were warned back by the men on the walk who had witnessed the uncanny accuracy of Ed's gun. Not a man moved for five long seconds, and then Dan Belden started obliquely across the walk toward the tie rail beyond which stood Ed's pony.

When Dan stood in front of him, Ed jerked his head back to indicate the two horses behind. "Unload that last jughead, Dan. Have a look at what the first is packin', but let it alone."

Dan said tonelessly — "Damned if I will!" — but moved a second later as the audible click of a drawn-back hammer from the gun in Ed's left hand came to him.

He caught his breath as he moved out into the street and made out Slade's body roped to the saddle in the outer shadows. Then he approached the pony with the pack saddle, and his hands went in under the tarp and felt the gold sacks. A moment later his fingers trembled as he untied the knots in the rope and caught Slade's body as it slid from the saddle. He was plainly bewildered when he glanced up at Ed.

Ed said — "Carry him into the saloon." — and Dan slung the body over his shoulder and moved in toward the walk again.

As Dan gained the walk, Ed swung lithely aground, his guns keeping in line with the fragment of the crowd still standing to either side of the doors. He drawled — "Everyone inside." — with an insistence that made them obey and move in through the doors immediately after Dan.

When the walk was clear, Ed looked down along the street. It was empty. His glance, swinging back toward the saloon's doors again, stopped when it reached the hotel verandah. There, clearly outlined by the light coming from a window behind her, stood Nan Hunter. Ed called: "You too, Nan. I want you to hear this!"

For a moment he thought that she hadn't heard him. But then she came down the two steps from the verandah and along the walk, stopping even with the saloon's doorway.

"What are you going to do?" she said in an even voice. "Haven't you done enough already?"

He said tonelessly — "Go on in with the rest, Nan." — the deep hurt inside him at the coldness of her tone not showing in his voice.

She gave him a long grave look and stepped inside the saloon.

He moved across the walk to the corner of the saloon wall and along it to the side window. Looking in, he caught the tense expectancy of the crowd near the doors. The men in there were eyeing the doors, and here, at the outer edge near the side wall, he saw two men who held guns in their hands. Across the room, lining the bar, stood Dan Belden and Tom Hunter and the men of the posse who were grouped around Ben Frost. The rest of the crowd was scattered in among the poker lay-outs on the side nearest the window. A few had taken chairs. A few more stood alongside the three pushed-together tables where the bodies of Prall's men lay. Slade was out of sight.

Ed stooped and picked up a rock twice as big as his fist. He threw the rock into the window, and, as the glass splintered and crashed to the floor, half a hundred men wheeled toward this side of the room at the sound. Those with drawn guns turned quickest.

Stepping back into the shadows, Ed called: "Maybe you ought to throw your irons away before I come in!"

He saw the glances of the two men who held the .45s narrow as they searched the shadows outside for a target. Not finding any and sensing the menace in Ed's tone, they dropped their guns. Ed approached the window, kicked out the ragged shards of glass along the lower sash, and climbed in through it.

He saw Nan Hunter standing at the far end of the doors and gave her a single brief glance before he eyed her father, saying: "Hunter, ask Dan what that other pack horse carried in here."

Tom Hunter's cold glance swung around to Dan Belden.

Dan said — "It's the gold, at least part of it." — and at his answer the strained attention of every man in the room riveted on Ed.

Ed took a sideward step that put him out of line with the window and with his back to the solid wall. With his guns hip-high, lined, he asked: "Where's the gent you lugged in here, Dan?"

Belden nodded to the floor at his feet, and the men between Ed and the bar moved out of line so that finally he could see Slade's inert shape lying in the sawdust a foot out from the long counter's rail. He said flatly: "No one's going to be hurt unless they make a try at me. Hunter, put some whisky down Slade's throat and bring him to. I think he'll talk."

"About what?" Hunter asked belligerently.

"About the rest of your gold. I was in that camp tonight before your posse shot it up. Slade was guard. When the others were asleep, he made me the proposition to double-cross the rest of the bunch and take the gold out." He glanced at Ben Frost. "Sort of spoiled your play, didn't it, Ben?"

Ben Frost looked surprised, then puzzled. He said blandly to Hunter: "I've never seen this man before. Who is he?"

Tom Hunter was plainly bewildered. His

face flushed in anger. He looked at Ed and said: "Thorn, this had damned well better be straight this time." He gave Dan Belden a curt nod, indicating Slade who lay on the floor nearby. "Get that man onto his feet."

The bartender passed across a bucket of water and a bottle of whisky. Dan unceremoniously upended the bucket in Slade's face. The cold water brought a quiver from the gunman's body. Dan knelt alongside him, propped his head up, and poured some whisky into his mouth.

As Slade gagged and caught at the bite of the fiery liquid, Ed thought of something that made him say: "One more man ought to be in on this. Where's Prall?"

Dan looked across from where he knelt beside Slade, saying derisively: "You still workin' that line, Thorn? Hell, Prall isn't here, never was."

"Where's the man who was passin' out the free drinks at the bar tonight, before I broke out of that jail?" Ed asked insistently.

As Dan Belden was about to reply, Tom Hunter said tartly: "Where is Fowler? He was here a minute ago."

"In his room at the hotel," a man near the door answered.

"Go get him," Ed said flatly.

"And take someone with you," Hunter

added. He eyed Ed coldly, speaking a thought aloud: "I'd give my last dollar to know how straight you're puttin' it, Thorn."

His attention was taken by Slade, who had put his hands on the floor and pushed himself up to a sitting position. Slade shook his head to clear his fogged senses. Then his glance strayed over the nearby faces and finally across the room to take in Ed. His shadowed face turned ugly in a grimace of anger.

"Take a look behind you, Slade," Ed drawled. The gunman, now halfway understanding the position he was in, turned his head until his glance met Ben Frost's.

"Slade, you're within an hour of feeling the hang noose, unless you talk," Ed said, speaking at the exact moment he figured Slade would see the insurmountable odds stacked against him. "Your gold's out front, ready to be turned over to its owners. Those shots we heard before I hit you cleaned out your gang. You're the only man left who can tell these men who Ben Frost is, who he works for."

Slade's head came around. He smiled thinly, came to hands and knees, and rose to a standing position. His glance went to the back of the room, where two of the sawmill logs still lay shoulder-high in the broken wall. For a scant second it was plain that he was considering what chance he had to escape through that opening.

Evidently the presence of men farther back along the room ruled out this possibility in his mind, for he looked back at Ed, saying arrogantly: "Why should I talk?"

"Because if you do, I'll personally see to it that you get a horse and ride out of here tonight."

"The hell you will!" Tom Hunter's deep voice boomed.

"Hunter, Slade's the one man who can tie this thing together and give you the proof you want. Do you want to find your son's murderer? Because if you do, Slade's the only man who can find him for you." Ed paused, letting that sink in, then queried: "Now will you let Slade go . . . if he talks?"

Hunter said in a low voice: "If he can do that, if he can show me the man that killed Bob, I'll let him go."

"Slade," Ed said. "Tell them who Ben Frost is."

Slade stepped back from the door, putting more distance between himself and Ben Frost. Then his level measured tones were striking across the room's expectant silence. "Frost hired me and the rest to come up here. We stopped a few stages at first, until we found no gold was going out. So he said we'd force the claim owners into shippin' it out. We raided a few claims, beat up. . . ."

The men to either side of Ben Frost had relaxed their vigilance in their intentness to catch each of Slade's words. Suddenly Frost slung out his arms in a broad and powerful sweep that pushed the men aside. A split second later he had whirled in behind the nearest man, snatched the gun from another's holster, and was swinging the man in front of him as a shield, his back to the bar.

Ed started to cry out when Frost's gun exploded in a burst of sound that was deafening. Slade's two hands clawed upward and ripped his shirt apart at his chest. Then, eyes bulging, he gasped chokingly for breath, took two lurching steps toward Frost, and all at once fell slowly face forward to the floor. The force of his fall made his body roll over once. A last convulsion drew his knees into his stomach and then stretched him out rigidly in death.

Held transfixed by the sight of an unarmed man cold-bloodedly shot down, no one but Ed noticed that Ben Frost had moved the six feet to the far end of the bar until Prall's man called loudly in a grating, harsh voice: "I'm goin' out of here! I'm takin' this man with me. He gets a slug in his back if one of you moves to stop me!"

His arm around the man's chest, Frost

moved back along the bar, his gun rammed in the man's back. Ed's attention was on Frost, as was everyone's in the room for the next three seconds. Then, all at once steps sounded on the walk outside and a smooth, bland voice from up front said: "What's the trouble here?"

Ben Frost stopped short. Ed's and half the glances in the room swung sharply to the swing doors. Bill Prall stood there, outfitted in his black suit and clean-laundered white shirt. His long face was creased in a frown as he stared into the half shadows toward the back of the room.

He nodded to the men who stood near him, one to either side, and said in that same unruffled voice: "These gentlemen tell me I'm wanted here." His glance had singled out Tom Hunter.

"Watch it, Prall!" came Ben Frost's explosive, damning words of warning.

Ed saw the blind sudden rage that welled into Tom Hunter's face. He saw, too, the savage mask of hate that crowded out the suave confidence of Bill Prall's look. In that instant of hearing Ben Frost's voice come out of the obscurity of the room's rear, Bill Prall must have realized the bitter irony of circumstance that had brought him here, entirely unsuspecting, to have his man give his identity by the mention of his name.

But Prall stood motionless for only the bare interval it would have taken a man to draw in a shallow breath. Suddenly he whirled, his right hand snaking in under the lapel of his coat. It came out fisting a blunt-nosed .45, and, as his hand moved, he took one quick turning step that carried him across toward Nan Hunter.

Ed saw instantly that Prall intended using Nan Hunter as a shield in the very way Ben Frost was using the man at the back of the room.

He cried stridently — "Down, Nan!" — and saw the girl's instant understanding of his word. Instead of falling, Nan ran toward the front end of the bar. Prall reached out wildly to catch her arm, missed, and then whirled to face Ed, whose presence he hadn't been aware of.

Once his target was clear, Ed thumbed back the hammer of the gun in his right hand, timing his move precisely to the downswing of Prall's weapon. Back along the room Ben Frost's gun exploded deafeningly, and a stab of searing pain coursed up along Ed's right forearm. His hand went loose, and the gun fell from his grip.

As he lunged aside, Prall's and Frost's guns spoke in unison. A concussion of air along his cheek told him where Prall's bullet had gone. The blacking out of one of the room's two lamps, the one almost directly over his head, marked Ben Frost's target.

Prall's shape was blotted out by sudden shadow. Before Frost's shot brought the remaining lamp down in a shower of broken glass, Ed had quick sight of Prall dodging for the swing doors.

He cocked the gun in his left hand as the room was plunged into darkness. He was watching the dimly lighted twin rectangles of night-lighted openings above and below the shuttered pair of doors. He only vaguely heard Tom Hunter's warning, strident cry — "Hold your fire!" — as the stage owner sensed the killing power of bullets fired wildly into a room packed with men.

Then, sure that the doors were clear, Thorn saw the rectangle of light above them broken along its bottom line and knew that Prall was on the way out. He thumbed two quick shots at the doors and heard a dragging step come on the heel of the explosions along the walk outside. He shouted — "Stay back, everyone!" — and lunged across the room toward the doors in long strides that had him elbowing the panels outward a bare three seconds after his shots.

As he wheeled out of the doorway, he had a

momentary glimpse of half a dozen men out there flattened against the saloon's front wall. Then the quick pound of a pony's nervously striking hoofs sounded from the near tie rail, and he looked out to see the black gelding he had ridden in rearing under the pull of sharply jerked reins.

Bill Prall's flat, high shape sat the black's saddle. A burst of powder flame leaped out at Ed from Prall's gun. He felt the impact of a bullet along his side above his hipbone as the horse came down on all four feet, wheeled, and lunged out into the street. His right arm hanging uselessly at his side, he swung up the gun in his left hand and laid the sights on the racing target that was Bill Prall.

He shot once and saw the man's vague shadow melt from the saddle as the horse veered sharply aside, pitching wildly. He ducked under the tie rail and ran out into the street, clear of the nervously prancing horses along the walk, his side aching with almost unbearable pain at each long stride.

Hardly was he clear of the horses when a gun laid its deafening echo into the momentary stillness. Ed targeted the powder flash of that gun and emptied his weapon surely, swiftly timed, in a rocketing crescendo of sound that was slapped back by the cañon's climbing walls. Blended with his own shots he

266

was aware of others and of the renewed flash of Prall's gun. When the hammer of his Colt clicked on an empty shell case, he felt suddenly weak and helpless and tossed the weapon out into the street.

A long training in caution gave him the impulse to step back behind the horses at the tie rail, for darkness blanked out the effect of his bullets, and each moment he expected Prall to fire again. But all at once he realized that his will couldn't summon the strength to move. Along with the pain in his right side came a new one high up toward his left shoulder. He remembered the bullet's blow coming as he emptied his gun. The pain was so blinding that it fogged his sight and the power of his brain to shape coherent thought.

Then, powerless to help it, he felt the muscles of his knees ease against his weight. He was falling. He struck the ground on his injured shoulder and wanted to cry out at the welling flood of pain that crowded in on him, but that cry came as a barely audible groan as unconsciousness crowded in on him.

CHAPTER TEN

When thought returned to him, he was first aware of a gentle, swaying motion, broken now and then by a harder jar that interrupted the smooth rocking of the bed upon which he lay. Gradually he defined familiar sounds, the clink of doubletree-chains, the softer creak of harness, the unrhythmic beat of horses' hoofs on hard ground, and the occasional ring of an iron tire against rock.

He opened his eyes and found himself staring upward at the faded upholstery on the underside of a Concord stage's roof. He recognized the pattern of that upholstery although it took him a full minute of concentrated thought to remember where he'd seen it. With the coming of the knowledge that this Concord was owned by Tom Hunter, a flood of memory poured in on him that laid a tenseness through his long frame.

"Dad, he's awake."

Nan Hunter's rich and musical voice somehow eased the bitterness of those memories, and he tried to turn his head in the direction out of which it had sounded. But pain along his neck muscles prevented that. A moment later her head came into his line of vision as she leaned across and down to him.

Her smile, the moistness in her eyes, glad of expression, at first puzzled him. Then a slow, settling throb of pain along his left side gave him the answer. A bed had been rigged between the seats of the stage, and he had been tied down on it so that the stage's motion wouldn't let him move against his wounds.

He saw Nan's lips move, heard her say in a low voice: "I've waited a long time for this, Ed. To tell you how wrong I was."

The sheer tormenting thankfulness that was in him at the meaning behind her words was broken by Tom Hunter, calling loudly: "Dan, pull in! He's come to!"

There came the sound of brake shoes grating against the tires, and shortly the stage had rolled to a halt. Ed could no longer see Nan but felt her presence beside him. At the limits of his vision he saw the door swing open and then Dan Belden's homely face was staring down into his. That face wore a wide smile.

"Feel like talkin', Ed?" Dan asked.

"Feel fine," Ed answered, a trifle bewildered at the fact that he could raise his voice only barely above a whisper.

"That's more like it," Dan said. "Tom, ease off those straps and sit him up so's he can look around."

Half a minute later Ed was lying back against Tom Hunter, who had his arm around him. He could see Nan now, take in the picture of her loveliness, her oval face, each detail of which he would remember always, the wavy highlights of her ash-blonde hair. But it was her eyes that spoke most eloquently to him, eyes that no longer mirrored loathing and contempt but a deep-running emotion he wanted to believe and somehow couldn't.

"You've got to get caught up on a few things," Dan Belden said as he took the seat at Ed's feet. "First, we got the gold back, every damn' ounce of it!"

"How?" Ed asked, his voice stronger this time.

"Frost. He made a run for it last night and had a leg busted by a charge of buckshot. Spilled the whole works when we carried him across the street to swing him from one of the rafters of that new store."

"And Prall?"

Dan's face took on a sober look. "Now there's something you should have seen. So full o' holes his carcass'd do for a sand screen."

"Dan!" the girl protested, yet she didn't shrink away from Ed, and her smile didn't change.

"Tom got straightened out on a few things, too," Dan Belden said. "Prall was so sure Frost would never talk that he told him all that happened up in Montana. And Frost told us. So here we are. As soon as we get you down below and have a sawbones pull that lead out of your shoulder, you can begin gettin' ready to help Tom handle this two-bit business o' his."

"Today's the last run we make on the trial contract, Ed," Nan said. "Some of Dad's friends have offered him backing. We're getting two new outfits, a Barlow-Sanderson and another like this. In another month, after the rains are over and the trail is open for good, Ledge will be booming. You'll have a full passenger list every trip."

"Some other driver will, not him," Tom Hunter said gruffly. "Ed, we'll talk that over later. I need a man to manage the business, one who knows more about it than me."

Dan saw the look on Ed's face, saw that he hadn't heard what Tom Hunter said. He scowled at Hunter, coughed nervously, and said: "Tom, there's something up front I want you to help me with. A busted piece o' harness." He winked at Hunter, and he and the stage owner climbed out and down off the step.

"Ed . . . ," Nan said, as soon as her father's and Dan's steps had moved up beyond the stage, "Ed, will you stay?"

"Will I?" Ed made to lift his arms toward her but couldn't for the pain and weakness. Nan leaned down to him. Her lips met his, and in that moment he knew that all the bitterness, all the futility of living was behind him.

ABOUT THE AUTHOR

Peter Dawson is the *nom de plume* used by Jonathan Hurff Glidden. He was born in Kewanee, Illinois, and was graduated from the University of Illinois with a degree in English literature. In his career as a Western writer he published sixteen Western novels and wrote over one hundred and twenty Western short novels and short stories for the magazine market. From the beginning he was a dedicated craftsman who revised and polished his fiction until it shone as a fine gem. His Peter Dawson novels are noted for their adept plotting, interesting and well-developed characters, their authentically researched historical backgrounds, and his stylistic flair. During the Second World War, Glidden served with the U.S. Strategic and Tactical Air Force in the United Kingdom. Later in 1950 he served for a time as Assistant to Chief of Station in Germany. After the war, his novels were frequently serialized in *The Saturday Evening Post*. Peter Dawson titles such as *Gunsmoke Graze*, *Royal Gorge*, and *Ruler of the Range* are generally conceded to be among his best, although he was an extremely consistent writer, and virtually all his fiction has retained its classic stature among readers of all generations. One of Jon Glidden's finest techniques was his ability, after the fashion of Dickens and Tolstoy, to tell his stories via a series of dramatic vignettes which focus on a wide assortment of different characters, all tending to develop their own lives, situations, and predicaments, while at the same time propelling the general plot of the story toward a suspenseful conclusion. He was no less gifted as a master of the short novel and short story. *Dark Riders of Doom* (Five Star Westerns, 1996) was the first collection of his Western short novels and stories to be published.